Lily

Karl Diaz

ISBN: 978-1-914130-63-2

OTHER TITLES BY IMPSPIRED

It's Like Walking a Tightrope –
by Mary Farrell

Particle Acceleration on Judgement Day -
By Peter Magliocco

In Between Pauses –
By Amrita Valan

Beautiful Boy –
By Joseph Mykut

Marty & Irene –
By Justin Wiggins

Old Wood Shop –
By Charlie Brice & Jim Hutt

Immersed in Blue –
By Margaret Royall

"April's showers bring May flowers."

(Thomas Tusser, 1557, 'A Hundred Good Points of Husbandry')

Introduction

I started writing in 2007, when I was in middle school. I started and stopped writing several science-fiction stories, my favorite genre. I still have a few I'm actively writing, including a long series of books focused on the competing geopolitics of several nations and an alternate history focused on Native Americans. I hope to publish the first outings of these in the next few years. When I entered the third year of college, I wanted to finish one. This book was Lily and I completed it a few months after graduation. It is the second story set in a shared universe, with the first being a play I wrote in high school. The play focused on a grieving woman trying to remove her painful memories. I am expanding it into a full novella and hopefully it will be the next work I publish. I hope you enjoy my first published work! I am grateful to Steve Cawte and his team at Impspired making this possible for me.

Lily

Chapter I.

Lily awoke with a smile on her face. She rubbed her eyes and looked at the virtual display clock hanging above her bed. It stated that it was 7:47 AM on February 4, 2035 in bright, green lettering. She tightened the waistline on her purple pajamas and she leapt out of bed, staring at a fading New York skyline outside. The cascade of LED lights danced before her eyes and made her feel warm inside. She rummaged beneath her bed, looking for faux fur slippers to keep her feet warm. She found them and walked around her spacious apartment, filled with unusual curios from her mother's travels. There were tribal masks from Africa, obsidian spears from Mexico and tiger bones covered in Chinese writing; all encased in glass. They showed her the wonders of the outside world.

She sat down in a mahogany chair, one of many that decorated their kitchen. She activated the wall TV with her voice: "ON."

The screen brightened and flashed as the news came on. She grunted, it was always bad and never hopeful. She picked up the glass remote and whispered into it:

"Agent Phoenix." It was her favorite show, showing the life of a female American spy in China with plenty of action, romance and character. She lowered the volume, fearful to wake her mother. She came in late after Lily fell asleep. She laid back in her chair, watching as Agent May Yi fled from the Chinese authorities once again. Lily yawned, it was a rerun she had seen many times before. She wanted the new season to finish filming and be available for streaming. Her stomach grumbled, so she got up and tapped on the virtual screen in the kitchen wall. This awoke the Virtual Helper Assistant which greeted her:

[Hello Lily, what would you like for breakfast?]

"Fried eggs and a side of bacon."

[Stick out your tongue first.]

"But..."

[Lily your mother programmed me with your dietary restrictions.]

She did as she was asked, grumbling as blue waves of light covered her tongue. The machine hummed for a moment and the voice returned.

[Lily, you have too much sodium in your diet. You cannot have fried eggs with bacon. How about whole grain cereal with fruit mixed in?]

"Fine but flavor it with sugar."

[Lily...]

"Fine, I'm sure the fruit will do."

[As you wish Lily. The meal will be made in a few minutes. Would you like to watch some news while you wait?]

"No thank you, I'll watch an Agent Phoenix episode instead."

  She picked up the clear remote, choosing one of the older episodes in the series. It was one of the first she had seen. Her mother had explained some of the complexity that lay underneath the episodes. There were the themes of the Eastern-Western philosophical conflicts, the violent history between the two and the jockeying for power between the US and China in the current day. It made the show more engaging for her and turned the seemingly good Agent Yi into a morally ambiguous antihero. Suddenly her mother entered the kitchen.

"Good morning sweetheart. What are you having for breakfast?"

"I have to eat whole grain cereal and fruit…"

[Good morning Ms. Dunkel.]

"Good morning Vicky. Sorry, finish what you were saying."

"I had no choice. The VHA wouldn't let me eat anything else. It even scanned my tongue."

"Hey, I know this is hard sweetie but this is how things have to be."

"I know mom…I know."

"You're only fifteen, so I know that you don't grasp everything yet. Still, please understand that this is the only way to keep you healthy."

"I do mom…"

Lily swallowed the pills without complaint. They boosted her immune system and allowed her to leave the apartment occasionally. That was mostly for regular checkups at the hospital though and very rarely something else. She glanced in the mirror, feeling somewhat distanced from herself. She undressed, letting the tub fill with water as her mother prepared for work at the Williamson Corporation. However, she did so in her own bathroom. Lily could hear her shower through the wall.

As the tub finished its automatic filling, she slipped into the warm water. She turned on the sauna function, letting the warm, moist air fill the room. It always relaxed her and made her happy even when she was very sick. She put her shoulder-length, brown hair into the water and dove beneath it briefly. In its murky depths, for a moment, she could be anywhere. She could be anyone. She rose again, the tub draining slightly to prevent spillage. She looked at her pale skin as the medicated water did its work. It absorbed the dissolved substances and was much better than constantly swallowing pills, ingesting fluids or worse of all, needle injections.

She slowly fell asleep, her head neatly nestled in a smooth indentation carved into the design. The soothing cocktail of chemicals swam in her bloodstream and let her forget her worries. When she awoke, it was 9 A.M. on the wall display and the tub was draining slowly. Her mother was already at work. So she got up and wrapped a towel around her waist, drying off in the hypocaust. She grabbed fresh clothes from sealed plastic bags from the bathroom closet. She then left the bathroom to read one of the digital books that her mother had purchased for her tablet. Lunch was hours from now.

Lily turned the tablet off as she finished that part of the story. She found Lord of the Flies interesting, if a little slow. She had read it dozens of times, but she still found the tale intriguing. Prepubescent males trying to survive in what most would paradoxically call paradise, with their youth and inexperience inevitably leading to tribalism, violence and power-mongering. She sympathized with Piggy, the smartest of the bunch. They mistreated him and damned themselves by ignoring his wisdom.

Still it was strange to imagine being literally isolated from the world. To have its problems so distant that they were unimaginable. The thought brightened her mood and teased a little smile from her melancholic face. Suddenly, her alarm suddenly began ringing, it was lunchtime. She shuffled off the bed and headed towards the kitchen, wondering what she wanted to eat. Vicky would have to relax the dietary restrictions for this meal, because the doctors told her that lunch was her most important meal. It was when her body was naturally most energetic and needed fuel. Thus, it was her favorite time of the day. Dinner wasn't half bad either but she always had to have less because her metabolism slowed greatly by then. She laughed, considering what fattening up was like. Fortunately, obesity was a disease that she would avoid. She sat down at the kitchen counter, patiently waiting for Vicky to awake from its sleep. It did so quickly, greeting her warmly,

["Good Afternoon Lily. What would you like to have for lunch?"]

She bit her lip, thinking about it. "Give me a list of what you can make based on ingredients in the house."

["As you wish. I can make tandoori chicken, a hot bowl of noodles served with vegetables or grilled salmon served on a bed of linguini."]

"Aww…nothing like the hamburgers or spaghetti and meatballs like you made last week?"

[No, I am afraid that you polished off those dishes ma'am. I can order them online but that will take a few days and we are trying to keep your sodium levels low."]

"I remember; how could I forget? Fine I'll have the tandoori chicken then."

[Excellent choice ma'am. The meal will take about twenty minutes to make. Why don't you watch Agent Phoenix or read one of your digital books while you wait?"]

"Will *do*…" She responded bluntly.

She crawled over to the counter once the meal was ready. The hot, steaming tandoori chicken was served with white rice and vegetables mixed within. She devoured it eagerly, reluctantly agreeing to Vicky's pleas to slow down. The chicken was spicy and savory in her mouth. It excited her and gave her face a gentle sheen of sweat. It took her less than ten minutes to finish the meal and she burped loudly in appreciation.

["Ah, so the meal was worth the wait."]

"Hardly, I've been starving while you slave away."

["Yes, you're welcome too Lily."]

Lily laughed and smiled at the comment. It was nice to have moments like this with Vicky. Even so, something was missing. She looked at the VHA and realized she was actually alone in the apartment every day. Vicky wasn't a companion, not really. She could provide what her body needed, but not what Lily wanted. A friend. Then it hit her why she always alone. She felt nervous to ask, sensing that it was a taboo subject, but she steeled herself.

"Vicky, did you know my father?"

Vicky remained silent for a few moments, as if considering it. ["How was Lord of the Flies Lily?"]

"Excellent and with social observations applicable to modern life. Now don't change the subject and answer the question."

Vicky was silent again, but eventually spoke,

["Yes I knew him Lily. He was an…interesting man, a complex man with a tragic fate. I didn't know of him for long. I also never met him personally."]

"He had Gutermuth's like me?" Lily implored.

["Yes he did. He unfortunately also passed it onto you."]

Lily started tearing, barely managing to ask, "So when did he die then? How old was he?"

["He died at 45 Lily. The disease slowly ravaged his body before he succumbed to it. He fought it for years though and medical treatment helped. It also presented itself much later than usual."]

Lily burst into tears. She bawled and shouted,

"So I'm doomed to live his life? To struggle meaninglessly and then die young?!"

[No. No *sweetie*…medical science has advanced greatly since then. Back when he was alive, Gutermuth's was novel and all its treatments were experimental. Now, they are far more effective at prolonging lifespan."]

"So I've got a chance then, a chance for a normal life?" She said, wiping tears.

["Of course. You've got a great life ahead of you. I wager that by the time you reach your father's age that it will be manageable."]

"Really?" Lily asked excitedly.

["Yes, now go off to the jungle gym and have some fun. Don't worry about your future just yet. Let me and your mother do that."]

"Ok." Lily did as she was bid, dashing off to the giant playset her mother built for her in the apartment.

April exited the taxi and paid the fare automatically, using the credit line attached to her fingerprint ID. Work had kept her late. She sighed, taking in the cold, city air while shadows and light danced around her. She walked into her building, waiting for the retinal scan to finish while slightly mesmerized by the glowing neon signs within. She got through and passed a dozen closed shops on the ground floor before entering the elevator. She tapped in the code for her private floor. She inserted her keycard and pressed the lit-up floor number. She was whisked up immediately.

The elevator doors opened and she stepped out, a paper notice falling out of her purse onto the floor. She picked it up, staring at it and momentarily remembering how she felt when she received it at work. So much time, so much effort just to see another delay in the case. She shook her head; it wouldn't do any good to worry about it now. She stuffed it back into her purse, awkwardly filled with her other things. She keyed in the combination to the closed-off, bone-white room in front of the door. She entered and put her purse down inside the decontamination chamber.

She sealed it behind her, stripping to her underwear and closing her eyes. She was sprayed with a series of antibacterial disinfectants. When it finished, she casually put her clothes back on, noting with mild distaste that they were somewhat soggy. She would need to reduce the ratio of water in the sprayed solution. She pressed her thumb to the door scanner, opening it quietly.

It was long past Lily's bedtime and April hoped that she was asleep. She turned the lights onto their lowest mode and crept past the kitchen and living room, hoping to avoid awaking Lily.

"Mom is that you?"

April cursed silently to herself, but the sound came from the living room not the bedroom. Perplexed, she turned around and gazed upon her daughter. Lily tiredly looked back at her from the couch and struggled to wrest herself awake. April smiled at her, lightly brushing Lily's hair as she sat down.

"Yes sweetie, it's me. What are you doing up so late?"

[She was waiting for you, but fell asleep.] Vicky answered.

"Oh did she now? Well tell me what couldn't wait until morning?" April playfully asked.

Lily stared into her eyes, twitching mildly and fidgeting in her grasp. April found it discomforting that Lily was so nervous around her, but waited until Lily found her voice.

"I asked Vicky about daddy and she told me that he died from Gutermuth's just like me."

So she knew, but how *much*. April continued smiling, showing none of her unease.

"What did Vicky tell you exactly?"
"That he died at 45, after years of fighting the disease with treatments."

April held Lily's face tenderly, wiping a tear that trickled down. She inwardly sighed, it had been years since she thought of him.

"Yes he did. He was such a brave and intrepid person, intelligent too. Just like you."

Lily buried her face in her mother's bosom, lightly sobbing. April held her close, buoying her from grief.

"Don't be sad Lily. You had nothing to do with his death."
"But I inherited Gutermuth's from him, didn't I?"

April paused for a moment, remembering the past. It was painful to recollect, even so long after his death. So many memories, many of which were heartbreaking. Still Lily knew none of that and she would know none of it. She would remain pure. The past was the past. April spoke softly to her,

"Yes sweetie, but that doesn't make it your fault. It's just...bad luck."

"Yes, but I'm such a burden. I tie you down to this apartment while never being able to go anywhere or do anything myself. Its…like I'm trapped here."

Lily was crying violently now, rocking her mother back and forth. April sighed, she was exhausted and couldn't think of any answer that would satisfy her daughter. Still she managed her best.

"No, you're not my burden. You are my *blessing* Lily. A reminder to cherish life always…"
"Really?" She asked, wiping away her tears.
"Absolutely. Yes. You are the center of my life. Now, we can talk of your father another time, but you and I need some sleep. Can you be strong for mommy and do that?"

"Yes mommy, I can…I love you."

"I love you too." April said, embracing her warmly,

Lily walked off to her bedroom, her steps seeming to alternate between certainty and doubt. She smiled back at her mother before slipping into the bedroom and shutting the door. April finally relaxed once she was certain Lily fell sleep. She held her head in her hands, wracked by quiet sobs of painful memories and regrettable choices. Lily was smart and naturally become curious, especially she spent most of her time up here in isolation. April got up, sauntering over to Vicky's main interface console.

"Hello Vicky."

["Hello Ms. Dunkel, would you like something to eat or drink?"]

"No, I need you do something for me."

["Yes, anything ma'am."]

"Keep quiet about details on Lily's father. I'll tell her myself if she asks."

["Ok, so what should I say when she does ask?"]

"Just say that you don't know any further details and that she should ask me. I'll tell her when she's ready."

[Anything else, Ms. Dunkel?"]

"No, good night Vicky. Deactivate."

Vicky obeyed and April passed her daughter's room, desperately seeking the comforts of her bed.

Lily awoke late, finding her mother already gone for work. Still, it was 8:30 and her mother could always arrive late because she was an executive or something. So why didn't she say goodbye? An awful thought came to her, maybe because she shouldn't have asked mommy about daddy. Maybe she was ashamed of Lily's weakness and avoided her now because of it. She teared a little, but she stopped quickly, wiping them away.

She slowly entered the kitchen, bypassing Vicky via avoiding her motion sensors. Her mother rarely left her in alert mode and usually she stayed asleep unless prompted. Lily knew what she would say and she wanted to eat something special. She pressed the button on the stove and a few minutes later out popped rehydrated hot pancakes drizzled with syrup and a side of bacon. She carefully tiptoed out of the kitchen into the living room. She wolfed down the meal, casually viewing an episode of Agent Phoenix in the background. After she was finished, she headed to the playset for some much-needed fun and exercise. However, she noticed that the door to her mother's room was slightly ajar.

She was tempted to enter it but her mother had forbidden it long ago. She always locked the door whenever she left the apartment. Now though, that was not the case. How…interesting. She wished to probe the room, wondering what secrets it held…maybe something about her daddy. Still her mother's prior warning and their last interaction discouraged her budding curiosity. So she entered the playset instead, passing through the enclosure's glass door. She grappled on the monkey bars and used the slide a few times but it grew boring quickly. She had to *know* what was in that room. Still she waited a few minutes maybe even an hour until she felt brave enough to do so.

Inside her mother's room, it was neat and organized, far better than Lily could manage. Her room was constantly messy but she liked it that way, it expressed her inner creativity. In contrast, her mother seemingly let nothing be out of place. As she wandered the large room, she saw piles of neatly folded clothes, a freshly vacuumed floor and every exposed surface was clean and sparkling. She was impressed by her mother's attention to detail and admired what it meant about her: that she was a clean, coordinated individual.

It made her happy to know this and she made to

leave. However, she found a small slip of paper peeking out from beneath her mother's bedstead. She picked it up gently, not wishing to crumple or damage it. On it, in big, red letters, were the words: Dunkel vs. the Thompson Clinic. It was a notice of a delay in the trial between the two. Why would her mother be suing this place? She replaced the paper where she found it, tingles of fear and anticipation trickling down her spine. She left the room quickly, shutting the door behind her cautiously. She would find out what the Thompson Clinic was and ask her mother about it.

Chapter II.

Lily tapped away at the keyboard, searching the "Thompson Clinic" in her laptop. There were thousands of results, but she clicked on the first link. The website's front page was a pure white background with cute images of infants and hearts on it. Beneath its corporate title, it stated that it was one of the best fertility clinics in New York. She noticed that It wasn't far from the apartment and wondered what her mother's connection was with the place.

This byte of information intrigued her. She would ask mommy directly about it and take whatever punishment she divined. She was coming home early for the monthly hospital visit. Lily shuddered, remembering the last time she was there. She could still feel the phantom pain of the needle as it penetrated her arm. Wishing to purge the mental chills, she went to the fridge and grabbed a sugarless, artificial fruit extract juice.

She sipped at it idly, its designed sweetness palpitating her taste buds. She sat down in the TV room's couch. Its light, silken covers brushed softly against her skin. She heard her mother finagling with the apartment door and turned to it. She came in, the pungent stench of disinfectants emanating from her skin. She smiled lightly but Lily knew what that face meant: needles. She cringed, tightening her left arm muscles. Cortisol flooded her system and she fainted.

April rushed over to her.

At the hospital, Lily fiddled with the obtrusive breathing mask. Her mother insist that she wear it because of the hospital's other clientele. However, it was becoming excessive especially with the immune booster pills being effective. April sat flustered beside her and had been feeding her medicine ever since she recovered from fainting at the apartment. Lily sat patiently in the lobby, irritated from the constant flow of medicine and anticipation building within her. She knew that the genomicist was preparing the shot in one of the rooms. Her genetic illness required her to take it once every six months to reverse gene damage. Gutermuth's attacked her immune system and intestines, while slowing the destruction of dead or decaying cells. So this shot extended her life, however long that would be. Now she knew that she would probably live only half as long as everyone else…she shuddered, banishing the thought.

The doctor appeared, his face grim and expressionless, ushering them into the private room. He closed the door behind them and her mother lifted up her shirt and pulled down Lily's pants, exposing her pale back. The doctor pulled the shot out from his lab coat and inserting it into her lower spine. She cried out and gripped her mother's hand tightly. She gritted her teeth, counting the passing seconds as the solution was injected. It traveled up into her brain, swimming around in the mess of cerebral fluid. After a painful eternity, it was done. The doctor applied a healing adhesive, sealing up the small puncture wound and killing any bacteria present. April pulled up her daughter's pants, ensuring that the fit was snug. He then drew out another empty, hypodermic needle saying,

"All right, Lily we need to draw your blood to check if you've been maintaining your diet and if the drug is working. Extend your right arm please."

"No mommy don't let him! You said we only had one shot." Lily protested.

"I know sweetie but the doctors insisted on this today. We've been behind on getting blood checkups."
"But mommy…"
"No buts. I'll get you some ice cream when we go home. I'll be right here the whole time, as always. Ok?"

"Fine…"

  She cringed as it drew her blood, finishing in thirty seconds. He wrapped a small bandage around the trickling wound and left wordlessly. Lily looked to her mother, whom offered an awkward smile of reassurance as she took Lily home.

  April could see that Lily was weak and dizzy, as they zoomed up to their floor. She held onto April for balance, nestling in the folds of her pantsuit. She passed out quickly and her mother carried her in, holding her steady as the disinfectant shower did its work. Inside the apartment, she undressed Lily, fitting her with clean pajamas and tucking her in. She left the room quickly and turned out the light, blowing a kiss to her sleeping daughter.

She sat down in the living room, sipping idly at a hot cup of fresh coffee. She would need to return to work in an hour, but she could rest for now. Still, she reviewed the Williamson stock prices and scanned her email for a response from the company's CEO about her latest design. The pods were innovative; no company had yet gone as far as these could. Artificial reproductive technologies had been used since the 70s, but this was wholly different.

Finally, womankind could free itself from the burden of child-bearing. These pods would one day grow babies from zygotes to fully-formed infants. She had seen the prototype work with a donor embryo, but they aborted it before it came fully to term. It was no longer necessary and machine couldn't handle further development. Still, the experiment had proved that the technology could work. The only thing was that there was some still some kinks in the process. They had not yet studied how pods affected the development of functional organs because of the existing laws on human biotech. In addition, the artificial umbilical chord had required constant maintenance. It frequently broke and led to toxin buildup in the developing embryo. It couldn't sustain a fetus to full-term at this point and it was too costly to continue repairing for more than a few months.

Still April was convinced it would work one day. Childless couples and those whom wanted to avoid the illness of pregnancy could have children. All she needed now was the approval and funding from the CEO Mr. Barrett. There was nothing though, all her emails were either ads from her many credit cards, updates on other projects or memos on the upcoming department meetings.

Disappointed, she closed her laptop and stared at her phone. By now, the rush hour was mostly over and she could take the train into Manhattan without worry. She got up and checked on her daughter, briefly glimpsing her peacefully sleeping form. She smiled, gently closing the door and putting on the rest of her work clothes. She put Vicky in alert mode and left the apartment, hoping that she could get off work early and spend some time with Lily later.

Lily rolled out of bed slowly, waves of nausea assaulting her. Her head hurt as well, burning and tingling. She walked a few steps tepidly, feeling a lump well up in her throat. She coughed, trying to expel it, but nothing came up. It was deeper, stirring uneasily from her stomach. Her itchy eyes were watering and there was a sickening acidic taste in her mouth. She shivered, inching along out of her room towards the kitchen. Medicine…she needed medicine and/or food. Food was preferable but with the rumblings of her stomach, she didn't imagine that she could keep it down. It would still taste good though.

She exited her room finally, finding every effort she exerted to be exhausting. Still, this pain couldn't be worse than the revulsion she felt within. She hobbled over to the kitchen counter, struggling to move comfortably as the wrenching feeling grew. She shuddered, tasting acid in the back of her throat and her nose dripped mucus. She finally reached Vicky, tapping at her blindly as she failed to hold it back any longer.

She vomited explosively, sending bloodied chunks of half-digested food all over the floor and counter. She slipped in it, rushing to reach the bathroom before vomiting once more. She coated the carpeted walkway between the door and the kitchen with more yellowish bile. She felt like wrenching again, more urgently this time, so she rushed to the bathroom finally and flipped up the toilet lid. She vomited several more times before she felt empty and utterly nauseated, burning in her mouth and throat. She let a few bits of mucus and saliva pass through her lips before getting up weakly and closing the toilet. She flushed, shivering at what she just did.

She wobbled as she made her way to the couch, determined to watch Agent Phoenix. Anything would make her feel better now. She reached it after a few minutes of wobbling back and forth, barely avoiding a scrape from the coffee table. She collapsed onto the couch. She curled up but the pounding in her head convinced her that TV wouldn't help. She shifted in and out of consciousness, vaguely aware as Vicky sent cleaning robots to deal with her disgusting mess. She heard something uttered by the machine but couldn't make out full sentences.

["Lily…just….I'm….alling…mother. She'll…here soon…"]

She passed out, unable to hear Vicky's last words.

  April sat there quietly, observing as the aged but still virile CEO stared intently at another executive's newest product. They were testing an updated version of the nanotech-based *Amnesia* drug. They claimed that it avoided the "residual memory effect" of the older versions, but that was bullshit. Messing around with the neural connections that formed memories to delete them couldn't go well. Memories or at least parts of them were imbued into the subconscious once they were formed. After that, they were indelible.

 She knew, she had once tried to erase some of the memories from the time before Lily. All the drug gave her was painful headaches and panic attacks when the memories superimposed themselves on what she currently was doing. They resurged every now and again but the antidepressants she took helped with that. Still, she shifted in her seat uncomfortably, briefly checking the virtual display in her wristwatch.

"…and we insist that this version is ready for human trials. We have tested it successfully with mice in mazes, chimps with patterns and other animal subjects as well. So what do you think Mr. Barrett?"

The old man plaintively stroked his graying, cropped beard tinged with white and continued staring for a few moments before turning to the board. A silent message passed between them. He was not impressed.

"Gentlemen, what we have here is great potential but I have reservations with it as is. As you must know, *Amnesia* previously bankrupted its original corporate creators, the Memento Clinic. It closed their business for good fifteen years ago when it became clear that their miracle memory-erasing drug didn't do the full job. Instead, it left its victims traumatized as shattered memories resurged in real life and blurred the boundaries between the two. Dozens went insane and a congressional hearing was heard on the subject, beginning the passage of multiple laws limiting human biotechnology…"
"Yes we know sir…" The designer insisted.

Barrett held up his hand. "I'll let you know when I am finished…" He stated coldly.

"…As I was saying, laws limiting human biotech were increasingly passed and this company, a startup then, nearly went under. We only survived by expanding into the less-regulated Chinese markets. I want you to keep this in mind with your 'so-called' product."
"Sir…?"

"I do not approve testing of this drug in the States. However, feel free to test it on subjects from China. Their damned authorities will hardly give a shit as long as they are paid."

"Yes sir." The designer replied bleakly.

"And don't forget, send the drug stateside once you've proven beyond a doubt that it doesn't cause insanity. Otherwise, consider your career here and in human biotech finished. Nothing you've made the last few years has impressed me. " Barrett declared, smiling coldly.

The designer and his team of creators bowed meekly, smiling awkwardly as they exited the board room. April suddenly noticed the panicked alerts from Vicky on her watch, apparently, Lily was sick or something. She tapped to reply to them when Barrett turned back to the board, disdain etched clearly on his face.

"Is that the best we have people? Should I consider paying you less to compensate for the lost value and profit at the next shareholders meeting?"

 The board looked back at him blank-faced and silent. No one dared to challenge the senior-most executive at the company whom had worked there since the passage of the Morgan-Hawke Act of '21. April hesitated at first but spoke up, clearing her throat loudly,

"I have something sir." She said smiling. She would deal with Lily later. Vicky could handle whatever little crisis had happened in that hermetic apartment.

"Oh do you now, April? You know it's been years since I've seen anything new come out of your department. For a while there I thought you had died and no one told me." He joked, getting a few snickers from the other execs. April however seized up at that comment, swallowing a lump in her throat. She steeled herself to speak.

"I know sir, but this is really something. Sorta my baby…if you will."

"All right, call me intrigued. Feel free to show us April, don't leave us all in suspense."

She got up and moved past the other board members, placing her thumb on the conference room's fingerprint scanner. It registered her, April Green, in the company database and drew up the list of projects that she was working on. They appeared on the virtual, interactive screen that projected onto the wall. She clicked 'the Human Pod Project' and drew it up for the board to see. Instantly, a dozen images, reports and academic research self-collated on the screen and organized into groups related by subject matter. She clicked on the images tab first and began speaking as a slideshow of the pods played,

"Women have long been the litmus test for the health of a society. When women did well, society flourished and happiness abounded. When they did poorly, it meant that society was rotten inside and sick. Now this wasn't because the stereotypically feminine values of acceptance, love and compromise trumped male notions of dominance, rivalry and hatred but rather because females gave birth to the next generation. When infants grow up in hostile, unloving environments, they become unstable, unpredictable adults. They are easily manipulated by events, demagogues, and the like. However, what if we could avoid this by avoiding the burden of pregnancy?" April queried ecstatically, pausing for a moment.

"Huh…" Barrett quietly remarked.
"Introducing the first artificial wombs or the Human Pod Project…we'll think of a cleverer title once we get more funding." She stated obtusely, getting a few pity laughs from her audience.

"Right…so does it work?"

"Partially…the prototype has allowed an embryo to develop normally and faster at certain points, but we did not allow it come to term."

"Why is that?"
"The umbilical cord kept breaking and it proved too expensive to maintain. It seems that part was the most difficult to replicate. In addition, its technically illegal to do so."

"OK, but the machine you built works more or less?"

"Yes, if we constantly monitor it."
"Hmmm…I see. I find this *interesting* to say the least. I've got half a mind to fund it right now because I'm so damn curious to see if it would really sell. Still, we've got responsibilities to our shareholders, to increase the value of our stock. How would you justify this expense now to them in my position?"

"Me?" April inquired, pointing to herself. She paused again, considering the question. "I would state that we could grow embryonic tissue for stem cell research in the pods while we worked out the other kinks."

"Yes, but aren't current methods of harvesting embryonic stem cells easier and cheaper?"

"No, we can test drugs on the developing embryo and harvest new tissue from it much later rather than extracting from a deceased or damaged younger embryo. Also, it'll be less problematic with public outcry toward this research since we can grow our own embryos rather than extracting them from surrogate mothers.

"Huh,,,all right. You've got me hooked April. Tell me more." He said, smiling for once.

April smiled back. "Yes sir." She said happily, the smile wrinkles emerging from behind her thick makeup.

  April returned late, having spent all day explaining her concept to the excited CEO. Williamson already had a significant share in the biotech market but her idea had convinced Mr. Barrett to increase that percentage. He loved the baby pods, emailing the research and development team to whip up a usable prototype six months from now. They would demonstrate it at the next stockholder meeting. She was exhausted, but her genius had finally been recognized. She could stake a claim to history. Right now, all she wanted was rest. She passed through the contaminant filters absentmindedly, leaning on the installed guardrails as they meticulously cleaned her nearly-nude body. She entered the apartment, passing Lily asleep on the couch. She sighed, she would deal with her momentarily. She entered her bedroom, tossing her work clothes into the hamper.

  She changed her bra and underwear as well, it was Thursday after all and tomorrow was wash day. She slipped into a comfortable nightgown and sat on the edge of her bed, contemplating. It was late but she still wanted to spend time with Lily. She also had to know what happened to her today. She scarcely remembered to check her watch for the updates from Vicky in the cab but at this point she would just to ask in person. It would be better, though her gut twisted anxiously. Lily had been weak earlier and the doctors still weren't sure why, that worried her. She breathed in deeply and exited her room swiftly, her bare feet cringing upon touching the cold, wooden floor. She sat down next to her daughter, lightly stroking her hair and calling her name. Lily stirred, blearily opening her eyes while a disgusting stench wafted from her mouth.

"Mommy?"

April momentarily hesitated, disgusted.
"Yes…sweetie, it's me. How are you feeling?"

"Better, but my stomach still hurts. I hardly ate anything today. I also threw up a lot."

[I can confirm this Miss Dunkel…Lily threw up several times today. I fear that she may be very sick. She also vomited blood…]

April's eyes widened and her mouth contorted grotesquely. "What?!…ugh I should have checked those messages you sent me. Stupid presentation…"

Lily sat up, suddenly awake. "Wait you didn't come home because you were giving a presentation?!"

April looked down, speaking softly, "Yes…we should be *fine* though Lily. We did your bloodwork today and that should let us know what is wrong with you. OK?"

Lily crossed her arms. "How could you mom? I'm vomiting blood and you stay at work to tell your boss about one of your products? What's wrong with you?"

"Lily that's not fair. I'm the only one who can take of you and provide for your needs."

"You're hardly ever home, this machine Vicky takes care of me." Lily said, hurt leaching into her voice as she turned away.

"Really does she take you to the hospital? Does she provide you with doctors, medicine and love? No? Well then stop accusing me of not taking care of you. I provide everything you need and work long hours to do so!"
"So what's the point of all that if I never see *you*?" Lily said, choking on tears as she looked into her mother's eyes."

April sighed, ceding the point. "Ok. Fair enough, I'll take off more time from work and be with you. Now I know its past bedtime but do you want to watch Agent Phoenix with me?"

"Really?" Lily replied, wiping away tears.

"Sure sweetie but just one episode. Then off to bed."

"Ok." Lily said, smiling slightly.

April snapped her fingers, turning the lights and TV on. The giant wall screen fizzled briefly before the image resolved. Agent Phoenix came on immediately, paused from the moment Lily fell asleep.

"Good, let's start where you left off."

"No…no mommy. We should watch the new episode. I made sure that Vicky recorded it when I woke up briefly a few hours ago."

[That I did, ma'am."]

"Ok then. Vicky play."

 The episode played, depicting May Yi during the Taiwan-China Missile Crisis of 2026. She hurried down the docks, donning worker clothes while trying to find the Triad boss responsible for the accidental missile misfire. The two watched with anticipation as Yi used her contacts in the Beijing police to raid the criminal hideout, exposing the crisis to be a conspiracy between certain Triads and zealous, ultranationalist PLA soldiers resenting anticorruption measures against their superiors. Suddenly April's phone began ringing and she paused the show.

"Really, its 8:30 P.M., who's calling me now?" She still accepted the call, walking off into the hallway between the bedrooms. "Yes, hello?"

"Is this Miss Green?"

"Yes, who is it?"

"Hi, this is Lyra from Manhattan Metropolitan Hospital. I have some preliminary results from your daughter's bloodwork."

"Ok…this couldn't wait until *morning*?"

"No, it's urgent. I have to tell you that her glucose, lipid and sodium levels far exceed the acceptable range."

"Wait…what?! Are you sure?!" She queried, trying not to shout.

"Yes ma'am, that's the first thing we check for with Gutermuth's disease patients."

"Thank you…can you schedule a morning appointment with the physician? I…need to speak to my daughter."

"All right ma'am." The nurse replied, hanging up.

April shook slightly and she spoke in a weak, whispery voice,

"Lily, have you been eating right darling?"

"Of course, I promised you."

April slapped her daughter viciously across the cheek. "Don't lie to me CHILD!"

April drew a rivulet of blood from Lily's cheek while Lily began crying and begging,

"No mommy I'm telling the truth!"

"You still lie." She raised her hand again, staring Lily down, but stopped from hitting her. "Lily, the doctors just told me that your glucose, lipids and sodium levels are all unsafe. That means you've been eating food you're not supposed to! That's why you were sick today! Have you been deactivating Vicky? Don't lie to me again."

Lily kept crying but she cleared her throat of the sobs. She spoke, tears streaming down her face,

"Yes…I was tired of her telling me what to eat."
"Why, that's part of why she's here though sweetie." She replied coldly.

"She's just a machine mom. Why should I listen to it?!"

"Stop that attitude right now young lady! You have to listen to it because there is no one else that can care for you while I'm at work. Now, go to your room."

"But I haven't finished the episode yet!" Lily protested.

"I don't care! You could have died Lily! Go to bed, you're grounded. You will conform to a new schedule and you will no longer be able to edit Vicky. Now only I will do that."
"But mom?!"

"But nothing…go to bed."

April awoke weary, crawling out of her cold bed and heading into the bathroom. She looked into the clear mirror, seeing only tired eyes and years lost. She washed her face brutishly, gingerly applying a small, lavender hand towel to dry off. She combed back her hair, snipping strands that dangled awkwardly. She dyed the graying strands dark brown, sighing as she reached the pinnacle of her morning ritual: showering. She undressed from her light, evening gown and entered the shower, preset to her preferred temperature.

 A display on the wall reminded her of the appointment with Lily's chief physician. She tapped the screen to confirm and scrubbed her naked form thoroughly, letting the lukewarm water awaken her tired soul. She exited within three minutes, standard timing. She had to see him briefly before work. While she was a mid-level executive, her past shyness and her duty to her daughter had put her out of favor with the CEO. It also threatened her career as Barrett had so callously indicated yesterday. This pod design was the best thing she had actually worked hard on in several years. So she woke up at 6, giving herself an hour to spend with the doctor before work. She dried off in the hypocaust, squeezing her hair to get the last bits of moisture out. It was cold today, in the low 20s as the display showed and she couldn't get sick.

 She shaved her legs afterwards and applied a light makeup, hiding the wrinkles of age. Finally, she brushed her teeth with an auto-brush, exterminating the plaque that colonized her enamel overnight and the majority of her mouth's harmful bacteria. While she took artificial immune boosters to avoid infecting Lily, she never took any risks with her. She laid out her work clothes, the suit and the rest, and dressed quickly. She walked over to her bed wall display, tapping a series of commands to Victoria before grabbing her purse and work documents.

  She left her room, passing by Lily's slightly ajar door and hearing her peaceful breathing. She smiled for a moment but the feeling soured quickly. Her virtual wristwatch beeped so she quickly left the apartment, swallowing one of the many energy tablets in her purse and passing through the sanitizing threshold.

"Good morning Ms. Green, I'm glad you made time to see me."

"I always have time to see my daughter's chief physician. So what's the damage Dr. Bonaventura?"
"Unpleasant, she's been substantially diet cheating since her last check-up a month ago. It's going to have long-term effects."

"And?" April asked pleadingly.
"While we can't be entirely certain…I'd say with 70% probability that it has shaved years off her lifespan, possibly as much as five."

"God…" April said, choking on tears. "So she might only live to be 20?!" She said, shuddering.

"Yes ma'am. I'm afraid so…I can try to extend her lifespan with some experimental therapies if you like…"

"NO. She's already endured more than enough medical treatments. There's no need to give her false hope, I mean…her last years are going to be brutal anyways. All I'll care about then is good hospice care, not extending her suffering."

"So are you going to tell her?"

"No doctor, I will not. She's still a child, no matter how smart she gets. There's no point in stealing away her hope and vitality before the worst sets in. I'll let her enjoy the bliss of ignorance."

Lily awoke that morning late. She had spent a long time crying last night, her tears staining the white pillows dark-grey. She itched her weary eyes and stretched her tired muscles, finding only a whimper in her throat. Mommy had cursed for her eating forbidden food, but she had to…years of eating the same, approved food took a toll. Everything tasted the same. So she had to mix it up, just a little. There were so many tasty foods out there, but they were just beyond her reach. Her condition prevented her from eating them. Or did it? How much could she have before it…*killed* her? Did she want to know? No…she was being too dramatic. There was a low chance of death if she controlled her intake.

So she had to find a way around her mother's edit block on the VHA. Vicky was the only way she could get food into the apartment, as it would need to be prepared correctly to avoid harming her. She shivered, while the outside world could easily kill her, the inside was no less depressing and it certainly was an empty existence. She opened her tablet, searching for hacking tips on virtual helpers, "life hacks" of course. Vicky was meant to "help" so why would it ignore the wishes of its master?

 Lily scanned through page after page of nonsense, related to crap she wasn't interested in. Virtual porn? Cooking? Scheduling? This was basic stuff she could figure out, even if the info on porn was blocked from her viewing. She figured this out when she was five. Where was the resetting the helper tips or maybe an instruction manual? Ugh…utter nonsense until she finally found it. She devoured the information, gleaning the answer she was seeking. There was a hidden switch behind the interactive panel that enabled either adult or kid settings. She would simply need to flip the switch every once in a while and she could eat as she desired. She smiled greedily, imagining the taste. Still…she would have to hide it from mom. Was that right?

  Yes. She was wrong to keep Lily from what she desired. There was so little in her world that gave her happiness and her mother was wrong to deprive her of it. She turned off her tablet, getting out of bed. She headed into the kitchen, the main CPU and the only panel she could reach and manipulate. As she attempted to flip down the protective cover, she found it locked and inaccessible. She briefly considered trying to trick Vicky by waking her up when the screen suddenly lit up on its own,

["Hello Lily."]

The little girl jumped back a bit, her pulse spiking. "Hi Vicky…"

["I am aware of your attempt to change my settings as is your mother. I have been monitoring your Internet searches and all your activities in this household, providing her with updates."]

"No…" Lily replied, distantly.
["So you've been remotely locked out of interfering with my programming."]

"No! WHY?!"

["Because I was designed to keep you safe and cheating on your diet is the opposite of that. Here, please eat this approved breakfast."]
"Screw you Vicky!" Lily said, crying as she ran off.

 She had to get out, she had to escape. The front door? No, it was locked and the outside world was fatal without an immune booster. They were also locked away in a kitchen cabinet. Then there was nowhere to escape to. Unless…the bathroom, would her mother monitor that? She smiled twistedly, mom would have to be pretty sick to do that. So she entered the bathroom and closed the door behind her, hoping to evade Vicky's all-seeing eyes.

She drew a bath, slipping into it and remaining utterly silent, uncertain as to if she was being watched. Did it matter? No. As long as she believed she wasn't being seen, she wasn't. Her head was neatly fitted into the smooth tub indentation and her body gently bobbed up and down in the water. It was peaceful, calmly floating with the waves that lapped around her body. She breathed in deeply, imagining she was suspended over a deep, dark, empty ocean. The only person in a lonely existence cursed to remain above the waves. Unless…she slipped under, diving deeper towards some far-off place.

A place where she could be free. She saw dozens of strange and wonderful animals, brilliant colors, felt the cool of the deeper water as the sunlight left them… and then the choking sensation. She needed air, the water was compressing her lungs! So she swam upward frantically, rising above and splashing it over the tub's fringe. She coughed vigorously as she spat out swallowed water, her nostrils burning. The tub was then drained, by Vicky's command nonetheless, so she curled up and started crying softly again.

It was warm, a spring sun shone down on a sleeping mother. April stirred briefly, her eyes straining against the brilliant morning light. Her hands gently caressed the silken sheets, grasping them softly.

April got up and rubbed her swollen belly, smiling as she gazed upon her sleeping husband. His jet-black hair rested against the cushy pillows and he woke after she kissed him. He smiled back and lightly rested his hand on her belly, causing the baby to kick. April's heart skipped a few beats. Her cheeks grew red and she laughed, showing her gleaming white teeth.

"Hello Doug…"

"Hi April. Did you sleep well?""

"Certainly after last night I would hope so." She replied, smiling deviously.

"Yeah, well I did my best. You got what you paid for."
 April laughed raucously at that, her face turning red and her whole body shaking.
"Yes I did." She crawled out of the bed, putting on more than her light sleepwear and shuffling over to the bathroom.

"So we're seeing the pregnancy doctor today right?"
"Yes, that's correct dear. In about an hour or so. So don't take forever in there."

"I won't!" April said as she picked up her battery-powered toothbrush. She began scrubbing away plaque with the automatic device as the continuous, repetitive noise grew steadily louder. It became an alarm. She awoke with a start.

 Her crusted eyes blinked off pieces of dried gunk as her aching muscles strained to lift her aged body from the dusty bed. She flipped onto her back, briefly glancing to her right, and sat upright. She turned off the cellular alarm and moaned lightly, her body protesting being awake. She fought the feeling off, moving to the bathroom and swallowing a cleansing tablet and dental fluid. The light blue stuff trickled into her throat, sending shivers down her spine but eliminating all the microbial inhabitants that grew in her mouth last night. It had no detrimental effects on the body, so she swallowed it rather than spitting it out. She wiped her face with a warm hand-towel and absentmindedly brushed her hair as Vicky prepared the makeup. The helper's arms lightly applied a mask of the stuff, hiding deep crevasses in her skin and the wrinkles of her age. That done, she left the bedroom and sealed it behind her, only unlocked by her biometric signature.

She headed to Lily's room, still disturbed by Vicky's report on her activity. She had tried drowning herself! Why? Why now? She wouldn't let that happen and had Vicky install a more stringent, responsive monitoring subroutine for the bathroom. Her daughter wouldn't kill herself…April wouldn't allow it. She knocked on the door firmly,

"Lily, please wake up dear." No response.

She did it again, louder this time. "Lily wake up and open this door."

No response. "Vicky, unlock the door."

The door clicked open and April forced her way in, finding Lily hiding meekly underneath a pillow.

"What happened yesterday?" She asked, reaching for

Lily.

Lily recoiled at her touch. "Nothing mom…nothing at all."

"Lily don't lie to me. That's not the truth. Vicky told me that you tried drowning yourself."

"No I wasn't! I was trying to escape…escape from you, escape from Gutermuth's…"

April sat down on the bed next to her cowering daughter.

"There is no escape from either. You need me and I need you. Gutermuth's too will sadly always be a part of you."

"Why? What did I do wrong?"

"Nothing. You did nothing wrong dear. Just…*bad luck.*"

"Bad luck…why did you have me if Daddy had my condition? Why?!" Lily screamed.

"We didn't know we had the condition then. We conceived you before the disease was recognized."

Lily crawled out from under her pillow, burying herself in the folds of her mother's shirt.

"No…no. Is that true?" She asked, tears in her eyes.

"Yes my love. It is." April said, stroking her daughter's hair.

"That's unfair. That's wrong! Why would I be born before we knew about the disease?"

"I don't know sweetie. I don't know…" April said blankly, trailing off and staring into the distance.

"Do you even care? Gutermuth's will kill me one day won't it?"

"No…yes…one day…"

"Then why does it matter if I break my diet?! Why does living longer matter if its just more of this?"

"Lily, there is nothing beyond this. Our time on earth is limited and we only get one chance. You can't squander yours because life is difficult. Besides…I love you and want you to stick you around as long as possible."

"What about you mommy? Are you squandering your life, your time by taking care of me?" She asked, rubbing her red eyes.

"NO! Of course not! Why would you say such a thing?"
"Cuz I don't think I'm squandering my life by enjoying it. In *fact*, I think the *opposite*!"
"Well, Lily, sadly you're wrong."
"How do you know? Do you wake up every morning knowing that you can't eat too much glucose, sodium or lipids?! That'll you likely die before you're 40?! That you're a little girl born only to die young?!"

Lily screamed, her voice cracking as her face dove into the bedsheets.

"Lily listen to me!" April commanded but Lily was unresponsive.

["Ms. Dunkel?"]

"Yes Vicky what is it?"

"Lily has passed out. I detect low blood glucose levels in her system. She barely ate yesterday so I presume she has collapsed from exhaustion. She will likely be out for several hours. I can wake her if you wish but I would advise letting her sleep and intravenously feeding her."

"Yes…of course…prepare the IV drip for her. I'll attach it to her arm and head into work I guess. Send your medical data to the doctors though. Let me know if they want her to come into the hospital. This fainting spell and her bloodwork leaves me nervous."
["Yes ma'am."]

 April looked at her daughter one final time, gazing upon her pain-wracked face. She shuddered briefly and then got up, leaving the bedroom.

Chapter III.

The pungent stench of chlorine tainted the air. The steady, rhythmic pulse of the machine's beeping and monitoring awoke her, albeit gradually. Lily noted that her muscles were tense and a breathing mask was fitted neatly to her face. Her breath fogged on the plastic and she wondered how long she had slept. Her last memory was…an argument with her mother. She passed out in the middle of it, but how long had it been since then?

Lily struggled to get out of bed, feeling her sore muscles writhe weakly. She noticed quickly that she was restrained at the ankles and wrists. So, her mother had ensured she would not escape and she still wasn't free. However, at least April wasn't there nor was Vicky. That meant she could choose to some extent, however limited that was. She also noticed that she didn't feel sick to her stomach anymore, the IV attached to her must have helped her.

Still there was a bad taste in her mouth and it was dry, the saliva making disgusting, thick strands between her lips as she tepidly opened them. She stopped, deciding to take note of her surroundings. She was inside a plastic isolation chamber with a locked mechanical door. It had a keypad unlike her apartment's fingerprint scanner, likely granting the hospital some flexibility with the doctors and nurses assigned to her room. There were no windows here, meaning she was somewhere on the inside corridor of

Manhattan Metropolitan. The only light, besides the faded rays attempting to breach the semi-translucent plastic, came from an overhead dull UV light that colored everything light blue. It was however properly shielded and Lily's eyes were undamaged by its sanitizing power.

She sat up in the hospital bed, finally seeing a juice box with a plastic straw on the table adjacent to her bedside. She picked it up, stretching against the restraints to the maximal extent and began happily sipping at the delicious liquid. Suddenly, she felt a tingling sensation from the base of her spine that rose to her brain, a viscous pumping of fluid that overwhelmed her. She fell asleep.

When she awoke, she felt the cool, peaceful water lapping around her exposed skin. The water tasted sweet on her tongue and she opened her eyes. Strange…she was back in the apartment. Had she fallen asleep again? How insensitive was she to being moved while knocked out? Still, it was good to be here, this was the closest thing she had to a sanctuary, a solitary island floating in a vast ocean of misery.

She felt someone's fingers stroking her right arm and saw herself but not herself. This other Lily smiled deviously, teasingly playing with her fingers off Lily's right arm.

"Hello Lily, how are you today?" She asked, smiling cruelly.

Lily shivered, not knowing how to respond when

suddenly another appeared. This one sat in the tub with her, but was silent. Her face was pensive and her eyes narrowed as she looked upon the other two. She was naked unlike the other whom was clothed in a gray suit.

"So it's come to this then? Talking to yourself?" She shook her head, playing idly with the ripples the water made.

"I'm…talking to myself?" Lily asked the others hesitantly.

"No." The cruel Lily replied, waggling a finger in Lily's face. "You're just going mad, that's all!" She stated, laughing maniacally as her eyes turned into vacuous voids.

"NO!" Lily cried out, embracing her bathtub twin. The twin looked oddly at her and inquired,

"What do you want me to do? This is your delusion."

"Ah, this is a delusion…good then." She replied, sighing.

"It can't be good if you're…"

  She woke again, for real this time, surrounded by the beeping medical equipment and smelly chlorine. She sighed inwardly, looking up at the featureless ceiling and breathing rapidly. It was just a dream…only a dream or like a drug-induced fantasy. Something like that. Meanwhile, the juice box had spilled over, soaking the sheets and her feet.

It had taken them nearly an hour to see the doctor. Traffic was backed up going into the city and the waiting room was busy. April and Doug sat there patiently though. It was only a few months into the pregnancy and everything had been normal so far. Well…*pregnant* normal at least. The constant increase in breast and belly size meant that her clothes no longer fit her and the weird, infrequent cravings were certainly a distraction. It was always for fast food too and despite her husband's warnings, she always found it difficult to resist.

Still she did her best to limit it and found spicy food to be a delicious, nutritious alternative. She turned to him smiling, her bright eyes taking him in. His hand rested gently on hers but he seemed tense, nervous even. She was about to ask why when the nurse approached them.

"Dr. Bonaventura is ready for you now."

"Good, I was getting hungry just waiting here." April joked, but Doug only gave her a tight smile.

The nurse led them into the back, passing dozens of closed rooms. She turned to Doug and whispered,

"Honey what's wrong?"

He replied, "Nothing, just the jitters I guess. I've had a bad stomach ache the past few days. I guess I'm just nervous about the baby."

She smiled at him, grasping his hand firmly. "There's

nothing to worry about."

 The nurse opened the door to the examination room and the doctor was there, already waiting for them. The youngish-looking man shook both of their hands firmly, with tight lines and dark ovals around his eyes indicating that he hadn't gotten much sleep recently.

"Hello April and Doug. I am Dr. Bonaventura, but you can call me Tony." He said politely, gesturing to the examination table and adjacent seat.

They obliged and he asked, "So you're here then for your routine checkup?"
"Yes, that's right doctor." Doug replied.

"Tony…please." He insisted.

"Ok. Tony, we just want to check on the health of the baby." Doug stated, his hand tightening its grip on April's arm.

"Good. Now you've been eating healthy I presume?" He asked, looking at April.
"Well…I've got some bad cravings for fast food but I've done my best to eat spicy food instead."

His eyebrow raised. "Ok but be sure to limit that as well. A balanced diet is essential for you and your baby, plus it'll be easier on your body."
"Right…" April replied, smiling awkwardly.

"Ok, good. Anything else to cover?"

They shook their heads.

"Good, well I'm going to draw some of your blood

April and a little from the fetus as well, just checking on hormonal levels and such…"

Doug tensed, his face a mask of pain as his hands tightened around his stomach and he lurched forward.

"Honey what's wrong?!" April demanded desperately.

The fit passed quickly, but his face was deep red and he leaned back uncomfortably in the chair, shaking a bit. April turned back to Tony, noting that his eyes had widened and he had stopped writing in his little pad.

"We'll take a blood sample for you as well. You're the father right?"
Doug raised his thumb weakly, "Yes…sir."

"Is that necessary? He's just got a bad stomach ache." She asked nervously, rubbing Doug's left arm.
Tony remained tense. "Yes, unfortunately that's one of the symptoms for this new disease we've been tracking."
"New disease?" April inquired.

"Yes. It appears that it is an unusual mutation being found in more parents and is being passed along to the kids…"

April froze, staring at him intently.

"…It's still fairly rare though. A blood test will rule that out."

"Ok then, well I guess…"

She awoke, catching herself after her head slipped off the desk towards the carpeted floor. Thankfully nothing was bruised but she spent a few moments recollecting herself. Fuck. She was dreaming of Doug again but where was she? Her eyes strained open and looked around. She was at work; she had fallen asleep at her desk working on the pods. At least she had turned off the computer first. She looked to her phone's lit-up display, it was 5 AM and work would start in a few hours. Just enough time to go home, shower, nap for a bit and then come back. Woohoo.

Lily awoke slowly, gently wiping away the gunk from her eyes. They had given her arms back as her condition improved and she was apparently responding to the medicine. Still…it didn't feel good to be tethered to this bed. She remained mostly isolated save for the few doctors in plastic suits that appeared randomly. They did their best to sound comforting, but in the darkened room, their faces were often masked in blackness. Thus, they appeared to be monsters of some sort, shadowy figures emerging from nothingness. However, Lily knew better and knew that human flesh lay beneath those plastic visors.

They had at least provided her with a small microphone, allowing her to communicate through an intercom linked to a receiver just outside the room. So she had had the occasional conversation with the nurses, somewhat soothing the loneliness. Still the hallucinations came every now and again, practically blending into real life. Her feelings on them had gone from primal fear towards mild acceptance. They were comforting, in a strange way. She awoke from her thoughtful reverie. Someone was tapping on the glass, violating the enclosed bubble of her existence.

She turned to the person, finding it to be a young boy. He looked to be her age and he was smiling as he pressed the button to talk,

"Hi, my name's Isaac. What's yours?"

She was surprised that he actually wanted to talk with her. Her face turned a little red but she replied, "Lily. My name's Lily."

"Hi Lily, I think I remember seeing you a few weeks ago. You were passed out and looked really sick…but now you look much better."

She smiled. "Thanks, have you been here long then?"

He looked down, being still for a moment. The smile quickly returned though, "Much longer than you. Umm…do you mind if I ask you a personal question?"

She turned away, gazing into the formless gloom. What did he want to know? Still, he was being nice and talking to her…so what could he ask that could bother her? She turned back, "Yes, go ahead."

He brightened up. "Do you have Gutermuth's?"

He knew what it was. "Yes, why? What gave me away?" She queried, smiling awkwardly.

"Uhh...the medical equipment and stuff. I mean…I have Gutermuth's too, so I know what the medicine they use looks like."

"Oh…are there other kids with Gutermuth's here at the hospital?"

"Yes actually, about a dozen."

She felt shy to ask, but something in her had to know. "Any girls, like me?"

"No…I've never met a girl with Gutermuth's before. It's all a bunch of guys. They're fun and all, but it gets old real fast." He said, winking.

She laughed. "It's fun though?"

"Yes, its good to be around people like us. It helps deal with the loneliness ya know?"

Lily turned away, barely managing, "I wouldn't know."

He replied reassuringly, "That's ok. When you get better and feel strong enough, I'll introduce you to the rest of the guys. I'm sure they'll be ecstatic to see a girl for once."

"Really?" Lily asked, blinking away tears.

"Yes, I'm sure."

"OK…I…" She brushed her hand against her waist, feeling something sticky between her legs. She pulled back the sheets and felt it, it was blood. Dark, sludgy blood coming out from between her legs! She cried out to Isaac, "Isaac I'm bleeding and it won't stop. Find a nurse for me!"

His eyes widened and he ran off, hollering for a

nurse. She clenched her fists. Why did this have to happen? He was so nice and she was actually enjoying their conversation. What was wrong with her? The panic grew and surged in her, causing her breaths to quicken and her pulse to rise. Was she dying, how would she know? How cruel. She passed out, consumed by the inky blackness around her.

They looked at each other, blank-faced and shaking. Bonaventura had just left them, his face tense as the results were revealed. They were both positive for Gutermuth's. Doug had the mutation and was gradually expressing it while April was a carrier. The bright day now felt mocking and lifeless, the dull overhead lights hardly illuminating the room. They both breathed unevenly and April struggled to find words to say,

"I think we should…*keep* the baby."

"Wait…what? Why? Just like that?! You heard what Bonaventura said! What kind of life would that be for our child?" Doug asked in shock.

"A life we can provide all the comforts for. They'll want for nothing! You'll keep your job as a lawyer and I'll go back to school for my master's in business administration…we'll hire a nanny to take care of the child."

"So we'll never see our child. She or he will grow up alone and cut off from everyone. Our child will never experience the joys of being outside or social interaction with other children with the weak immune system and strict dietary restrictions they'll have! I mean fuck April! I'm dying from this disease right now and I don't even know how I'll adapt to it."

"We'll do it together. I'll help the both of you cope…"

He snorted. "*Coping*…what a life that will be."

"It's better to be alive than dead!" She insisted.

"Yes but a good quality of life is nonnegotiable. Otherwise that's not true! I don't have a choice in the matter, but our child does. We have a choice. We don't need to burden our child with a miserable life here. We can abort the child and adopt instead."
"You want to murder our baby?!" She screamed.

"*Murder*? Since when did you become an anti-choicer?"

"I'm not but this is our child we're talking about. It was born because of us, our love." She said softly, reaching for Doug.

He withdrew, staring at her harshly, "It's a twisted symbol of our ignorance. We can't let it come to term when we know how miserable it'll be for its entire life."
"No. You don't know that." She rebutted, shaking her head.
"Oh I do. I do. No child wants to grow up cut off from everyone else thanks to circumstances beyond their control. I know I have hell to look forward to and I can't stress how fucking wrong it is to bring such a child into the world. To let them grow up with this

disease and struggle painfully for years, all while deprived of meaningful human experiences."

"There will be a nanny." April insisted.
"Oh will there? How will she deal with the child's weak immune system?"

"I don't know…let's cross that bridge when we get to it."
"We are CROSSING THAT BRIDGE! We can have the child now with the disease or abort it to spare it the misery. We can adopt a child instead!" He countered.

"Damn it Doug! Why do you have to fight me on this?" April inquired, tearing up.

He sighed and went over to comfort her but she pushed him away. "NO. I won't abort our child. I was so happy to be a mother until a few minutes ago. Now, I still won't give up on our baby. It's ours, a product of our love. I won't let it die unless you are willing to let our love die…"
"What are you saying?"

"I'll divorce you Doug if we abort this child. I won't let it die without letting our marriage die." She stated forcefully, tears streaming down her cheeks.

Doug breathed in deeply, looking down for a few moments before returning to her face. "Fine. You win. We'll have the baby. When it grows up unhappy, miserable and despising us, don't accuse me of letting *our love* die."

"So you're back?" The Twin asked drily.

"Oh I missed you!" The Other said sarcastically, embracing Lily and kissing her.

"I didn't miss either of you…why am I here?"

"My guess it's that you need someone to talk to and that someone is us!" Other replied, laughing gleefully.

"Yes. I cannot contradict that. It is true." Twin stated.

"So let's talk then about what recently happened." Other ordered.

"No…uh…we don't need to do that."

"Really? But that boy Isaac was so *cute*. I mean the whole you freaking out, bleeding everywhere and it just being menstruation was *pathetic*, but we can avoid that topic."

"Excuse me! If I didn't know what it was, you didn't know what it was. You are a part of me Other."

"Other, that's really your name for me? Please, I could think of a better one." She replied laughing.

"Nope, I created you so that's your *damn* name!"

"Whatever you say, *boss*." She said smirking.

Lily glared at the suited monster before turning to Twin.

"Twin, anything you have to add on the implications of menstruation?"

"Well you can have a baby now and you overreacted to

the news."

Lily frowned. "Not exactly what I meant but…OK. I mean…I'm still trying to accept that."

"Yes. Through puberty, you will develop as a woman. I cannot tell you what that entails exactly since you don't know."

She smiled tightly. "Thanks, I'll keep that in *mind*."

"So Isaac then?" Other queried.

"Yes Isaac. I like him but…ugh…what do you think of him?"

"He's nice and kind, but we shouldn't spend time with him. Your immune system remains weak and unlike him, you haven't interacted with people with Gutermuth's for years. I don't see socialization going well."

She nodded sadly, turning to Other.

"Oh me?" She asked deviously, pointing to herself. "I think he's kind but we should absolutely pursue a relationship with him. I meant we feel something, right? We should pursue that feeling wherever it leads."

"That's illogical…I don't…"

"Shut up Twin. Let Lily talk." Twin obeyed, albeit with noticeable hesitation.

"Thanks…I guess. I'll heed Other's advice in this case."

"Yay! Now there's another matter I'd like to discuss."

"Yes?"

"Have you ever wondered how sex happens?"

"Well…yes. I'm too young to have to worry about it though."

"Perhaps, but have you realized why people do it?"

"No."

"Come on, you remember that scene from Agent Phoenix, that passionate embrace between Agent Yi and her counter spy…April made you cover your ears and close your eyes, but that didn't stop you from hearing and seeing some of it right? Those passionate moans, the way your heart leapt as Fai kissed her…do you know why you liked it and why people like sex?"

"No…"

"It's because its pleasurable, that pleasure must be so intense. Now, why do you think that you bled from…down there? Other asked, prodding at the space between Lily's legs.

"No. I mean I menstruated but…"

"Well ask one of the nurses when they come back huh? I'm sure the answer will be…*enlightening*."
"I will." Lily replied, the illusion dissipating. Her eyes opened and she saw a nurse there. She made to open her mouth, but realized that the nurse was staring at her with wide open eyes. She wondered why when the nurse suddenly ran off, a chill rushing down her spine.

April tinkered with the device's wiring, ensuring that it received sufficient power to pump the blood around and to keep the artificial placenta alive. The device was crude, larger than necessary to grow a baby, but it sufficed for now. It was oval in shape and about the size of an office chair, a bioplastic viewing window in the upper half of its design with several readout monitors scattered around the surface. This would allow the technicians to service it and adjust levels of oxygen, iron, nutrients, etc. as necessary. It was also cloaked in warm, low lighting to simulate a natural womb as much as possible.

Inside the device was an innovative, hybridized interface of machinery and biology, an experimental cyborg tissue that generated artificial amnion and kept the developing fetus at an ideal temperature. This interface was nearly as difficult to successfully replicate as the artificial placenta. Both proved to be limiting factors for the pods and prevented them from allowing a zygote to grow to full term. However, for the purposes of growing embryonic tissue for stem cells more rapidly and testing drugs on developing fetuses, it would work. They just needed to carefully maintain it and learn from their mistakes. It had already taken a decade of research and refining to reach the pods, so April imagined it would be a few decades yet until the devices were ready for a more commercial application of growing infants en masse.

Still the artificial blood pump and cyborg interface were valuable inventions by themselves. They would be eventually sold after Williamson officially patented them and demand went up. One day, women would no longer need to endure the trials of pregnancy: the bloating, cravings, incapacitation, bodily damage and the *joy* of childbirth. She shivered, remembering her experiences, and was glad to give other women the opportunity she never had. Age wouldn't matter if the eggs were harvested early enough and the baby could be born whenever it was convenient rather than when it wanted to come out.

Plus, if it really took off, they could design a new baby formula that built on the growth nutrients the infants were exposed to in the artificial wombs. They would grow faster, live longer and be smarter than their peers. At least, that was the ideal she strived for. For this to occur, they would need to bypass the difficulties with the placenta and uterine wall by making the machine more biological than mechanical.

Suddenly, her cell rang and she walked off, letting her technicians continue to work.

"Hello, this is April Green."

"Good afternoon Miss Green. This is Lyra from Manhattan Metropolitan. I'm calling in regard to your daughter Lily."

"Yes?" She queried, irritation seeping into her voice.

"She's been doing well and recovering from her poor diet but there's been a...*disturbing* development."

"What happened to her?" She demanded, concern

mixed with anger in her tone.

"She's been hallucinating for a while now. We noticed a few weeks back after she woke up but its appearance has increased in frequency. We were wondering what you would like us to do. I'm sorry I didn't let you know sooner but we thought…considering her *upbringing,* that perhaps that it was best to tolerate the hallucinations."

 April held her phone, utterly still, shocked beyond words. Lily was hallucinating…*why*? What did it mean? Was her mind degrading that quickly? But it had taken so *much* longer with him? The accusatory tone in Lyra's words just infuriated her more.

"Is there anything that could have caused this beyond the diet? Any change in her surroundings that might have affected her psyche?"

"Well…no, not exactly." Lyra replied hesitantly.

"Not exactly? What do you mean?!"

Lyra sighed. "Lily has been interacting with a boy at the hospital, a fellow Gutermuth's patient. They've been speaking to each other for the last week."

"How?"

"We installed a microphone intercom system for her room. It lets doctors and nurses interact with her safely and efficiently."

"It also allows unauthorized individuals to converse with my daughter." She didn't have time for this so she considered her options quickly and opted for the simplest solution.

"Prevent this boy from interacting with my daughter any further. No one, but the medical staff may speak to her until I see her first. Is that understood?"

"But Ms. Green, there has an uptick, an improvement in Lily's health recently. Fewer hallucinations even." Lyra insisted.

"Is that guaranteed to be from her time with the boy or could it just be her body responding to the medication?"

"We aren't completely sure. Normally Gutermuth's patients never reach this critical state so…"
"Are you accusing me of being a bad mother again? I am her legal guardian and I choose the method of treatment for her!"

"Fine…just remember that if a lawyer challenges this and uses the Dunkel Precedent against you…well the hospital is not liable."
"Understood, goodbye." She hung up immediately. She would have to schedule time to see Lily soon. Mr. Barrett had had them working on the project intensely so she hadn't had much free time at all. Still Lily was essential to her and she would make the time. She had to.

Lily was napping peacefully, wrested from sleep by the repetitive calling of her name. She opened her eyes, squinting as she saw one of the nurses on the microphone. It was Lyra, wasn't it? She sat up and replied to the nurse.

"Yes, what is it?"
"You have a visitor Lily. A lawyer from Anson, your father's law firm."
She noticed the dirty blonde woman standing next to Lyra. She wore a bright smile and a crisp suit. How interesting. "Please send her in."

  The nurse quickly fitted the lawyer with an isolation suit. The lawyer entered and helplessly tried to adjust the in-suit microphone until Lily pointed to the correct knob. The lawyer smiled at her and sat down at her bedside.

"Hi Lily. My name is Abby. You probably don't know me, but I knew your father very well."

"I see…what was it like working with him at Anson? What was he like?"

"What was it like…*Right*. It was very fulfilling working for Mr. Dunkel. He started me as a paralegal in his office and helped me rise through the ranks. He was a good, honest man…a man that struggled to do right by people."

"Hmm…so you were his friend then? I wonder what that's *like*."

Abby blushed. "Yes, it's why I'm here Lily. I've learned of your predicament and how your mother has blocked you from seeing a boy here, even though talking to him has improved your health."

"Yes, I want to spend time with him. Still, what can you do for me? She's my mother and makes these decisions for me."

"Well, I intend to use something your father created. It will let you choose your treatment. It's called the Dunkel Precedent."

Lily's eyes widened. "Really?"

"Yes. It's essentially a special right for only Gutermuth's patients. It lets them seek better treatments if the existing ones are failing. It even lets children override their legal guardian's preferred treatment since so many patients are children."

"Are you sure this will work? *Why* are you helping me?"

"I am not completely sure, but there is a high chance it will succeed. I am helping you, because I feel I owe it to your father. To do this last good thing in his name." Lily started crying happily. "Thanks…I don't know what to…"

"GET AWAY FROM HER, BITCH!"

Lily froze, turning to the window. It was April and she was very angry.

"Screw you April. I'm not going to let you *fuck* this one up."

"I am her mother you whore. I'm sure Justice Steele will side with me on this. Now, Lyra get her lying, cheating ass out of there."

Lyra sighed. "As you wish."

She escorted Abby outside the sealed room. Through the glass, Lily watched and barely heard the growing argument between the two of them. Hospital security forced Abby to leave and April glared at Lily through the window. Lily cowered under her stare.

Lily awoke much happier. Lyra told her she could finally leave the claustrophobic room, cloaked in a kaleidoscope of darkness. Her health had improved enough and she could spend time with Isaac and his friends. Abby had freed her using the Dunkel Precedent. The judge ruled in Lily's favor. April had failed.

She smiled, finally someone who really cared about her feelings and helped her. She sighed, putting on her cleanest, prettiest outfit: a dress with pink flowers and blue butterflies, before exiting the room. She tapped in the code and left, walking hand-in-hand with Isaac to the isolation chamber where the other Gutermuth's patients were kept. They were escorted by a pair of nurses.

"So how many other boys are there?" She tepidly asked.

Isaac smiled uneasily, "About 5-7, depending on the day. A few of them are real…*introverts* so they don't always show."

"Hmm...so at least I won't be most socially awkward then?"

"I mean we'll see…but it's not likely. I think they'll be *real* awkward around you."
"Why?" She asked, hurt in her voice.

He shook his hands apologetically. "I didn't mean anything by that. I mean they'll be awkward cause you're a girl and we never see any girls, save for the nurses I guess." He said, turning back to their escort. They gave tight smiles and rolled their eyes.
"That's right…you said that to me before. I'll follow your lead then Isaac."

He smiled widely. "Thanks, that's all I can ask for. Here we are."

The nurses entered the door's code and the two children entered the decontamination chamber. Lily felt the door seal behind her as a gentle spray of disinfectants coated her body. Lily closed her eyes but it wasn't necessary, the hospital only used specially-designed organisms for cleansing not chemicals. They would simply become a part of her body's microbial biota. Still, she closed her eyes since she loved focusing on the sensation of the droplets hitting her skin, it was surreal. She grasped his hand tightly as they entered the room.

It was completely sealed off, with only one entrance. The room was entirely white, with reinforced plexiglass windows and a few colorful images of kittens and flowers that radiated positivity. She smiled, at least it felt safe and no machine would tell her what to do despite the ubiquitous presence of small cleaning drones sweeping the room. The boys were all playing strategy games on a rectangular, waist-high table, each with a partner. They played chess, checkers and even wéiqí, with Lily smiling inwardly as she remembered that esoteric game of white and black stones from Agent Phoenix.

The boys looked up as they approached and were staring, clearly just at her but they said nothing until after she sat down.

"What do you want to play Lily?" Isaac asked.

"Are there only board games here?" She asked jokingly.

He smiled, "No, but we don't usually play with the toys anymore. We're too old for that and it doesn't pass the time well."

She gazed into his dazzlingly hazel eyes. "How long are you usually here?"

"We try staying for 12 hours. It's the only place in the hospital that's truly *safe* for us so we get up at 8 AM and leave at 8 PM. It limits the chances of us running into sick patients."

"Ah, well do you have another chess board then?"

"Yes we do, I'll be right back." Isaac said, heading to the toy bin on the other side of the room. He began rummaging through it to find the board, apparently it was highly disorganized.

One of the boys scooted closer to her and asked, "So

you're Lily, where are you from?

"From Manhattan, uh…a few blocks away."

The boy smiled. "Interesting, how did you come to the hospital then? Were you transferred here?"

"No, I was living at home and then I got really sick, so I was taken here. I've been coming here though for as long as I can remember."

Another moved over. "Hmm…but you never lived here before?"

"No."

The two boys looked at each other and Lily increasingly wished Isaac would find the board and come back. "Ok, so have you ever been around *other* Gutermuth's patients?"

"No, I lived alone…well with my mother I guess."

They both smiled eagerly. "Nice to meet you then Lily. We hope to spend some more *personal* time together."

She frowned. "Ok, what's your name then?"

"Francis and this is my friend Hernan." He said gesturing to his partner.

"Nice to meet you!"

They laughed strangely. "Don't worry about it. It was *nicer* to meet you."
"Don't worry about what?" Isaac asked.

"Nothing Isaac, we're just getting to know Lily. She seems…like a *nice* girl." Francis replied.

"Yeah well keep it nice huh Frank? Or I'll show how *nice* I am." Isaac threatened.

Francis' eyes narrowed and he returned to his game of wéiqí, seemingly disinterested in her.
"So shall we begin?"

Lily turned back to Isaac, whom blushed as she stared at him.

"Yes, but I've never played against a human opponent before. Do you mind going easy on me?"

"Sure." He replied gladly, moving his first piece.

It started with the baby's kick. April stirred in her semi-conscious state. The baby wasn't due for a few weeks. She slipped back into slumber. She rested for only a moment, a painful urge emanating from between her thighs. Her body felt like it was being split. Fiery pain crept up and down in waves through her whole body. It stole her breath and tightened her abdomen, making her fight to say anything. She eventually cried out loudly, awaking Doug.

"Wha…what's wrong babe?" Doug sleepily asked.

She stated irritably through gritted teeth. "It's the…the baby. I'm ha..ving contractions!"

"Oh *shit*…I'll get ready. You need…uh…nicer clothes?"

"Can you see my cunt?"

"No…"

"Then I don't need nicer clothes. Now GET READY."
She commanded.

He obeyed, rushing out of the room. She tightened
her fists and tensed her muscles, desperately trying to
breath between contractions. It felt like a tire was
pressing down on her abdomen and that burning coals
were being pressed to her thighs. Her sweat soaked the
bed through and based on the sounds outside of the
room, her husband couldn't find the car keys. She
cursed, trying to find something to distract her. She
heard a tap at her window and the taps increased in
frequency.

It had begun to rain, apparently the cold embrace of
March was finally giving way to a warmer, wetter
April. The rain calmed her for a few moments, but that
searing pain overwhelmed her eventually. She
hollered, "Doug, where the fuck are you?!"
He burst in. "I'm here, I'm sorry babe. I couldn't find
the keys with these tired eyes. I worked late last night
and.."
"*Don't* make fucking excuses. Just get me to the
hospital!"

"Yes ma'am. Posthaste."

After ten minutes of ramping up and cooling down of
that ecstatic torture, she was in the car with her legs
braced tightly against the floor. She tried breathing to
no avail, the pain only intensified. In addition, the rain
was picking up and traffic was grinding to a halt on

the road ahead. While April grasped the car door handle with superhuman strength, Doug turned on the radio for local traffic and raised the volume as the rain became a steady, powerful beat.

"Good Morning New York City. It is a dreary, rainy day here in Manhattan and of course, traffic is building up on both the local roads and the highways. The rush hour traffic is really slowing down and it seems that on several roads morons have gotten into bad accidents, clogging up the road. Now we'll…" April turned off the radio.

"Hey I was listening to that!" Doug protested.

"Yeah, I wasn't. It didn't help, I already *know* traffic's bad. All I want to know is how long it'll take us to get there. What does the GPS say?"

Doug shrugged tensely. "It keeps updating slowly, so it started off at like 30 minutes, now it's like an hour."
"Ugh…"

"Sweetie, I know this won't help you but it will help me destress from your *bitchiness*. You're the one who decided to have the baby during morning rush hour…"
"DECIDED?!"

"…and we'll get there when we get there."

Two hours of agony later, they arrived at Manhattan Metropolitan. She was ushered into the hospital in a wheelchair while Doug screamed,

"Woman in labor! My wife's in labor! Move! I need

help!"

 Even in her dissociated state, April shook her head as nurses helped her onto a gurney and into a room. It took nearly six hours of pushing and relaxing, shortness of breath and shouting, but eventually the child emerged. She had done it without painkillers as labor had started by the time she got there and she *paced* out the birth. April breathed in deeply for the first time that day, looking out at the window and noting how the rain reminded her of her pulse now. A regular, gentle rhythm of pitter-pattering. Doug, whom she had the spent whole time either crushing his hand or yelling at him to calm down, had finally shut up. He looked the child over, freshly cleaned by the midwives whom had backed away to a respectful distance.

"Here it is. This is our baby." He said softly, a slight smile lighting up his face.

"Is it a boy or a girl?"
"It's a boy." He replied curtly.

"A boy? How about we name him...*Rain.*"

Chapter IV.

Lily looked at Abby, marveling over her pretty hair. She asked softly,

"Why are you *really* helping me? I'd like to believe what you said, but that doesn't make sense to me. I've had time to think about it. How would you even know who I am? How well did you know my father?"
Abby sighed. "You're an astute one. We worked together for almost two decades before he passed away. He and I were close friends for almost all that time. He told me about you."

"Okay, then why does my mother hate you?"

Abby looked stunned. She swallowed through and asked, "Has your mother never spoke to you about me and him?"

"No. My father's like a taboo topic and she's never mentioned you before."

She chuckled. "No, I guess she wouldn't. What do you know of your *father* then?"
Lily scrunched her eyebrows. "Almost nothing I guess. Uh, he had Gutermuth's too and died at 45."

Abby tensed, swallowing nervously. "So you don't know anything else about him?"
"No should I?"

Abby sighed. "No, I mean…I can tell you a little about him, but this is something you should ask your mother about. This isn't my story to tell."

"I've tried! April isn't telling me anything and she clams up every time I ask! Its why I'm asking you."

She looked over Lily critically, shaking slightly. "Your father and I were *lovers*…I was with him until he died. I was married to him for two years."

Lily swallowed nervously. "So he cheated on my mother?"

"*Cheated*? Hardly, there wasn't much love in their relationship for years. I guess technically…" She said, laughing emptily.

"So you're not representing my mother in her case against the Thompson Clinic?"

Abby's eyes widened. "No, how do you know about that?"

"A few months back, I snuck into my mother's room. I found this delay of trial notice on the floor and I saw that it was between her and Thompson."

"Ah. Ok…" Abby replied, sighing.

"Why is my mother suing the Clinic? Does it have anything to do with me?"

Abby was still for a few seconds. "She's suing the clinic, because she broke the law and still wants compensation. The clinic messed up too. I'm representing the Clinic as their lawyer. Now there's more to this, but you don't have to *know* it. You *shouldn't* know it. I mean…you're what, 14?"

"I'm 15." She replied meekly.

"You're still too young to know more. When you're older, say like 18, and if your mother still doesn't tell you what happened, I'll do it. You deserve to *know*. For now just enjoy your life. There'll be *time* to know these things."

Lily hesitantly nodded, but clenched her tiny fists. She turned away from Abby and curled up in the blankets on her bed. Abby looked her over once and left wordlessly.

Rain rolled out of bed, his face red and his nose stuffy. He coughed loudly, feeling phlegm well up in his mouth. He quickly exited his room, barely aware of the commotion in the kitchen. He entered the bathroom, turned on the sink and spat it out. He cringed as the disgusting, green glob slowly dissolved down the drain. Then he repeated the action, six times, cringing a little less with each loogie.

He walked into the kitchen, finally registering the intense argument between his parents. It was the second one this week. He sighed, sitting down and pouring a bowl of gluten-free cereal while he tuned in.

"April this is unacceptable! You need to stay at home! He's used to your germs and not these babysitters that keep getting our son sick." Doug shouted accusatorily.

"Wow, takes balls for a man to admit nowadays that he prefers the stay-at-home, 50s wife. Well too bad! I'm in the workforce and I'm not going back home. Who's going to take care of you? Who's going to pay for your and Rain's medical bills if I stop working? You can't keep working forever." She retorted, pointing at Rain.

Rain nodded wordlessly. Hmm, how nice. Usually his parents took longer to acknowledge his presence, although it didn't stop them from arguing in the first place. Why though? At the surface, it was because he had gotten sick while being watched by his babysitter, Sandra. It wasn't her fault that it happened, she was so nice, but his immune system was just so weak. Still, it had prompted another passionate clash of words. There were deeper issues at stake and through his careful listening, he grasped why they really argued.

His mother was struggling in her career in the biotech sector while his dad was succeeding as a lawyer, despite Gutermuth's steadily progressing. He looked him over critically, noting that while he seemed strong, subtle cues gave him away. When he shook while being still, it showed neurological damage. When he coughed and swallowed antibiotics like candy, it compensated for his immune system. These were the things he had to look forward to as he grew up. Still, his was manageable at this point and only kicked in occasionally. His thoughts returned to the crisis at hand, remembering a nearly decade-old film he had watched online without his parents knowing. It depicted the spread of a chimeric virus spreading from China throughout the world with millions dead. While it pained him to see it, reminding him of both his vulnerability to disease and inability to see the outside world, it gave him a useable solution here. To avoid being infected, the scientists wore plastic containment suits while they worked with the virus. He cleared his throat and interrupted the argument,

"Excuse me, mom? Dad?" They both stopped momentarily and looked at him.

"I have a solution that can prevent this from happening in the future."

Doug looked back at him curiously while April tensed her shoulders and gazed at him skeptically.

"Yes, what is it?" She asked coldly.

"My babysitter can wear a transparent, plastic containment suit when she's here. While it normally protects the wearer from the outside, now it will protect me from the wearer."
Doug nodded silently, smiling a bit. April looked at him unflinchingly and asked,
"So where did you get that idea from?"

"A movie. Cont..Conta…Co…"

"*Contagion*." She corrected. "So, you've been watching things behind our backs huh? You'll be losing your Internet privileges for a week then."

"No mom!" Rain protested.

"No buts. It's a good idea however and I think we should do it." She stated, looking at Doug.

His dad's face clouded with anger momentarily and then calmed. "Don't make me the bad guy April. You're the one punishing him for being curious. He's

13, but he's not a child anymore. Gutermuth's ages you and he's been learning his whole life. He's years ahead of other kids, in maturity and biology. I know, the disease has aged me as well. He shouldn't *suffer* for wanting to know more about the world outside this apartment."

"It's too dangerous. He can't go outside Doug without getting very sick! Why torment him with what he can't experience?"

"It's better to know than not to know. If I hadn't learned I had Gutermuth's by now…well I could be dead. I take so many antibiotics and sick days now. *Fuck*…if I didn't know."

"Doug, don't curse in front of him!" April demanded.

"April! Fine…you're right. Don't repeat that word Rain."

Rain nodded, a growing tightness at his core and in his feeble musculature. He made to speak up when the doorbell rang.

"Who could that be?!" April queried angrily.

"I don't know. I'll check…it's probably Anson." April recoiled at that comment, but Doug didn't seem to notice. Rain got up, having finished his breakfast, staring at his father as moved back from the eyehole.

"It's Abby, my paralegal. If she's here to fetch me, then something big is happening with the *Amnesia* drug." He sighed. "I forgot my phone was off. Maybe they need me for the negotiations."

He opened the door while April's eyes narrowed.

  A young, blonde woman with strikingly blue eyes and a shapely body walked in. She seemed nervous and shrunk in April's presence. She addressed the couple after a few moments of silence.

"I'm here…I'm here to pick up Doug, umm…Mr. Dunkel for the negotiations between Memento and the…FDA over the Amnesia drug. They've come to a stalemate…"

April glared at her, but said nothing. Doug looked at her, then at Rain and lastly replied. "Ok. I'll be there shortly Abby. Is the company car waiting in front?" She nodded, briefly glancing at April.

"Good tell the doorman I'll be down in ten minutes." She nodded again and left wordlessly. His dad stared at her for longer than he should have, particularly at her butt. Rain briefly looked up at his father, seeing something there. April exploded a few moments after she left.

"You're fucking that little *whore*, aren't you?!" April screamed.

"Hey you just said…"

"Shut up you little shit! Are you or are you not fucking her?! She yelled, starting to cry.

"No, I'm not sleeping with her."

"Good then you're staying right here and…"
"No. I'm leaving." He countered coldly, walking

toward the door. April grabbed his arm.

"What the hell are you doing?!"
He shrugged her off, "I'm going to where I'm needed and *appreciated*. Goodbye April. Have a good day Rain."

"No we will finish this argument…" He left her mid-sentence. As the door closed behind him, she cried out incoherently. She marched off to the master bedroom, tears in her eyes. Rain shook, feeling the tension in the room finally subside. He walked back to his room and curled up in bed. He stared at the wall and started crying.

  April arrived at the New York Supreme Court building thirty minutes early. It was a humid day in October, the urban heat rising rapidly. She was finally cashing in on some of her allotted vacation days. Hopefully, she could finally end the litigation between her and Thompson. These days were supposed to be used for taking care of Lily, but she was still in the hospital and April needed to take *care* of this. Nine years was more than enough. She scaled up the marbled white steps, crossing between the aged columns with the promise of justice engraved above. If only that were true.

  She entered the courtroom, thankfully no reporters were there this time. She strolled towards her lawyer, the jury settling in. Her lawyer stood up as she approached and was smiling at her. She smiled back and briefly turned to Abby, who glared at her. She flashed an unsettling smile and sat down. Abby would suffer for all this trouble soon enough. Several appeals to higher courts and stalled progress on her tort case would not dissuade her, but only make her more determined to win. She smiled inwardly as the justice sat down and brought the court to order.

He made his customary greetings, addressing the court, the jury, etc. He made the two lawyers approach the bench and reintroduce their briefs to him, giving their vague statements as to why either April Green or the Thompson Clinic should prevail. It wasn't anything she hadn't seen several times throughout the years. She fingered her legal dossier, containing all the evidence of Thompson's past malfeasance. Hopefully, this time, it would help. It also vindicated her actions as that of grieving mother. That much was true, but she hadn't imagined ever needing to sue them at the time. She made her choice, which was illegal yes, but it was best of the options available to her.

She stared idly at the justice and then at her lawyer, watching gleefully as Abby struggled to contain her anger. The justice seemed more frustrated than she was with the gridlock the case was in. At least April didn't mind waiting. Doug, if anything, taught her lessons in patience. She twisted her ballpoint pen around, maintaining a face of regal calm while inside she was dying of boredom. Finally, Abby called her to the stand as a witness and the justice cleared her to proceed.

"April Green, you have accused my client, the

Thompson Clinic, of medical malpractice. Is that correct?" She asked, ice in her tone.

"Yes. Several *times* at this point."

"Then you understand the hypocrisy of your accusation, don't you?"

"Excuse me…hypocrisy?! I went to the Thompson Clinic for a clean, artificial insemination so that I could have a child." April turned to the jury. "I had lost my only son shortly before I decided to go to the clinic."

There were a few sympathetic oohs so April turned back to Abby.
"So you knowingly went to a sperm bank despite being a confirmed Gutermuth's carrier and having already lost your son the disease, with your husband following a few months after the insemination?"

April tensed. "Firstly, the sperm bank injured me by failing to keep contract and provide me with a clean, anonymous donor that did not have Gutermuth's. Secondly, my son died of a drug overdose and my *ex*-husband, left me." She paused. "To be with you, *Abby*."

The jury went silent. April darkly smiled and Abby stared down at the floor, hair concealing her face. After a few moments, she stood up straight again and was smiling disturbingly.

"Yes, I took your ex, Doug Dunkel, as my lover. So what? He divorced you years before this, because you poisoned the marriage by keeping that bastard Rain instead of adopting. You then ironically lost Rain, lost

Doug and then birthed Lily by ignoring the Dunkel Precedent. You got impregnated despite having Gutermuth's. There is no *legal* thing justifying what you did and how it *turned out*. However, the Dunkel Precedent which Doug created, explicitly condemns your actions and was designed to prevent any future, legal Gutermuth's baby pregnancies. You privately bribed a doctor to impregnate yourself and you got what deserved for it, *bitch*."

April sneered. "How long did you get to enjoy Doug? I can't imagine a dying man could be much fun for what, a few years? I was married to him for *fifteen* years, beat that ya *whore*."

Abby lunged at April, glaring at her while they were face-to-face. The justice had his bailiff intervene and restrain her, but Abby cooled off quickly. As she was collecting herself, April spoke directly to the jury despite the justice's admonitions.

"As for the accusation of the private bribery, that is false. Thompson Clinic maintains a legitimate façade, but has deep ties to the biotech black market. My lawyer has a legal dossier with proof." She nodded to her lawyer, whom sent over digital copies that flicked onto the jury's small terminals. She smiled inwardly, she could see the confusion and doubt warring in their faces. She almost *had* them. Then Abby said,

"I have no further questions your honor. Please allow me to bring up my next witness."

The justice wearily nodded while April exploded

inside. She did her best to speak calmly.

"Excuse me Justice Steele, but I am presenting evidence to the jury. I don't think Abby can just…" The justice held up his hand.

"Enough, she can do that. The jury will continue considering your evidence as she brings another witness to the stand. Now please, go sit down."

April obeyed grudgingly, pouting inside while her lawyer sat there expressionless, in utter silence. She at least liked that, he knew her moods and when not to cross her. Abby then called her next witness, "I call Lyra Johnson to the stand." April perked up, Abby was using Lily's former nurse. *Fuck.*

Lyra walked past April, glaring at her the whole way. April just smiled back coldly, considering just how many times these women would be fucking each other over today. Apparently, a lot. She leaned back, both curious to hear her contrived BS and just a little afraid. Abby asked her the first question,

"What is your relationship with the plaintiff?"
"I used to be Lily's primary nurse and was for her entire life, working under her chief physician and an old-friend of April's, Dr. Bonaventura."

"How good of a relationship do April and Lily have?"

"It's very strained. Lily is deprived of almost any outside contact and has spent her entire life either at home alone in her apartment or at the hospital. April is also very overprotective and spends most of her time

working at the Williamson Corporation."
"I see, has there been any *incidents* indicating abuse to you?"

"No, not exactly. However, Lily is unusually withdrawn and I wasn't even sure if she could maintain a healthy relationship with another human being. That is, until she met Isaac. He's a slightly older boy at Manhattan Metropolitan that also has Gutermuth's. They get along nicely, despite my expectations otherwise."

The jury looked impressed, prompting April to sink further into her chair. She would need to look into this Isaac, to see if he was a bad influence on Lily. He was the boy Lyra mentioned weeks ago. Still he never would have interacted with Lily again if it hadn't been for Abby. She clenched her fists underneath the table.

"So, why is Lily at Manhattan Metropolitan?"
"She violated her dietary restrictions pretty badly and nearly died about a month ago. Thankfully, we saved her but still..."

"Yes, one can always wonder otherwise. So, the matter at hand. Why were you fired?"

"I was fired, because I went to you Abby once I heard that April was cutting off outsider access to Lily. I thought that was wrong and wanted to do something for this poor, vulnerable little girl who just wanted a bit of *happiness* in this world." She replied, tearing up.

April barely suppressed her disgust. What a manipulative *cunt*.

"That's wonderful. So they fired you specifically because…?"

"They fired me because I broke doctor-patient confidentiality. However, I felt it necessary to bring you in because of your vested interest in this case and since I felt that Lily could benefit from the Dunkel Precedent."

"I see. Thank-you. No further questions your honor." Abby sat down as April's lawyer hastily got up. April narrowed her eyes, watching as he nervously strolled to the stand and began asking his questions. She turned to the jury, noting how they had soaked up that emotional BS. She shivered, disgusted with their inability to separate emotions from facts. She rolled up her nice suit sleeves, considering her next move.

Lily moved her first piece, a pawn two places forward. Isaac smiled a bit, making the same move with a piece on the far left of the board. She followed it up by moving another pawn a space forward, before conversing with Isaac.

"So how was your um…*morning*?"

Isaac smiled. "Good, good. I mean…boring as usual, but nothing to complain about. You?"

"Same."

"Yeah now…I'd suggest you pay better attention. You just lost your bishop."

Lily frowned, his words dawning on her. "Isaac!" She

protested. "I'm new at this."

Isaac laughed giddily. "Yeah, well it's too much fun to not take advantage of your ignorance."

She frowned and stuck her tongue out at him. "Fine. By the way, you just lost your rook." She said, smiling deviously.

"Hmm…I guess I'll pay better attention too." He said distantly, moving his queen.

A sudden thought occurred to Lily and her stomach became queasy as she pondered asking him. However, she eventually gave in, as a part of her had to know.

"Isaac, do you ever think about your parents?"

"No, I don't. Why?" He asked, looking back at her.

"Um well…I never met my father and my mother and I…have…well…uh a *complicated* relationship."
He didn't look up. "I never met my parents. They were members of the urban poor and conceived me without knowing my dad had Gutermuth's. They were young too, if I remember correctly. Anyways…they couldn't afford the prenatal diagnosis and only gave me up for adoption at birth once they realized the mistake."
"Do you hate them for that?"

"No. I don't. They couldn't afford the medicine needed to keep me alive and I would have died young." He laughed awkwardly. "Well, younger I suppose. After that, I wasn't adopted and I've lived here ever since."
"Did you…did you ever look for them?"
"Yes, a few times, but I quickly realized it was

pointless. They're not really my parents and it's not like they could really see me, being a bunch of germy hobos and all."

"You don't think that's being too harsh?"

"No, like I said, they're not *really* my parents. No one was or is."

"Ah, I guess so." She nodded hesitantly.

They made to return to their game when Lily noticed that Hernan and Francis were staring at her and Isaac. He noticed too and spoke up loudly,

"Hey, don't you two freaks have better things to do? Go back to your game or I'll teach you manners with my fists."
Lily blushed. "That's not necessary…"
"I think for them it is. Creepy pu…" He stopped mid-sentence, swaying a bit. "Is it hot in here?"
Lily's eyebrow raised. "No, I don't think so. Are you OK?"

"Yeah why?"

"You just lost your bishop to my pawn."
"Really? Crap I need to pay better attention."

 Lily smiled and giggled, moving her queen absentmindedly. Isaac was such a nice boy. A ray of light and hope in her dark, dreary life. A person who she could trust and…that wasn't her controlling mother or that damned machine! She looked at Isaac, feeling her heart race and her cheeks redden. However, he was saying something to her and was jumping up and down excitedly.

"What…what is it?"
"You just lost your queen to my knight."

"Ugh…really?"

A few moves later, she had recovered from her huge mistake. Still nothing was certain and they had traded the more mobile pieces with each other. Now, she only had a rook and a bishop to defend the king, along with a half dozen pawns. She moved her bishop into an attack position but was crushed by Isaac's knight again. Swearing under her breath, she moved her rook into a subtler attack position. He reacted by moving his queen…nowhere near her piece. It was so strange that she temporarily unfocused from the game. She noticed that Isaac was shaking badly and sweating profusely. As she took his king, he hardly seemed to react. "Isaac are you…" He fell to the floor suddenly. Lily screamed and began banging on the glass, shouting, "HELP, he needs help!"

The nurses heard her pleas and quickly gained access, typing in their shortened password. They crossed into the room, wearing masks and gloves. They grabbed him and escorted him out of the room, with Lily close behind.

Rain coughed lightly, his nanny gently wiping the spittle off his chin and sanitizing the nearby area. She was cloaked in a plastic isolation suit, but it was colored pink and blue instead of white. He figured that the manufacturers thought that would make it more kid-friendly. It sorta did, but that really didn't matter. What relaxed him most was the person hidden beneath the suit, Sabrina. She was a gorgeous woman, curvaceous and yet very fit. Her smile made him feel warm inside and his hear race. He had turned 14 half a year ago and he could see why his father struggled to stay faithful to his mother. Abby was far younger and more attractive. Sabrina was even younger than Abby and at least he could *imagine*…maybe. His mother however, was a *bitch* to him and his father.

He sympathized more with Doug than April, since she was so controlling. His father was far more tolerant and he had to be, since he was also dying from Gutermuth's. His mother had the luck just to be a carrier of the disease. She knew nothing of what it was like to constantly be within death's grasp. Yet, she micromanaged him anyways. Ugh. He turned back to Sabrina, who was busily preparing his cough syrup and letting his soup cool on the kitchen counter. She smiled back at him and he turned away, his face turning bright red. She brought over the cough syrup, which he eagerly downed and placed the warm soup in front of him. He began devouring it, since it was his favorite: mushroom soup.

The warm, delicious taste awakened him from his cold and he noticed that she was staring at him. She sat back, watching and smiling. He only blushed harder and he hoped that she believed that either the cold or the warm soup turned his cheeks redder. He finished it quickly and she took the bowl away from him and washed it in the sink. When she returned, she lovingly brushed his hair back as gently as she could. How he enjoyed her touch, how he wished to feel the warmth of her fingers against his face. He closed his eyes and resolved to put these feelings finally to rest.

"Sabrina?"
"Yes?"

"I'm feeling sleepy, do you mind if I take a nap?"

"Of course, you don't need to ask for my permission."

He smiled. "I thought…it would be best to be polite." Now she blushed and his blood ran hotter in his veins.

"Thank you then. Let me tuck you in though."

"NO. I mean…I'm a big boy now. I can do it myself." He said, lightly puffing his chest out.

"OK, *big boy*. When you wake up, I'll be sure to put on your favorite show: *The Expanse*."
He smiled eagerly. "I'd like that. I'll…see you later Sabrina."
"See ya." She said happily, awkwardly waving to him in the suit.

  He closed the door behind and sealed it shut, as quietly as he could. He knew it wasn't really closed, but at least it made it more difficult for her to interrupt him. He turned off the lights and got beneath the blankets. He had looked up how to do this online previously and he was going to be as quiet as possible. He removed his pants and underwear, weaving his small hands around his slowly extending penis. He rubbed it up and down gently, gradually filling it with blood. When it was taut enough, he spat into his right hand several times and began rubbing it more vigorously.

Waves of pleasure came and went, shaking his tiny frame. He made sure to focus on Sabrina, tuning out all other distractions. Her dark hair, her startlingly blue eyes, her full, large breasts, the sweet red of her lips and her…firm, taut ass. He could tell she spent her free time at the gym, working her leg muscles. He fantasized her removing the suit, then the rest of her clothes piece-by-piece and lifting him up to her lips. How warm her embrace would be! How wonderful her lips would taste! And…and…he spasmed suddenly and unleashed his semen explosively. It coated his blankets and bed with wet spots. He sighed slowly, it had felt good, *really* good. It couldn't have taken him more than a few minutes, but he felt exhausted. He breathed in deeply and felt the restless longing of sleep take him.

When he awoke, his mother was already in his room, had flicked on the light and was screaming.

"Rain what the fuck are you doing in here?"

His nanny peeked in, over April's shoulder, but quickly withdrew. He could tell her face was red and it filled him with some satisfaction.

"I masturbated mom. So?"

"SO?! You shouldn't be doing any of that shit! You're...too *young*."

"I'm fucking dying from Gutermuth's and you're upset that I *came* too early?! I don't have a long life to look forward to mom, unlike *you*."

April's face turned bright-red and uglier than before, making angry contorted shapes.

She shouted, "Shut the fuck up! I am your mother and you will do as I say when you live in my house boy! What the fuck were you even jerking off to? Was it her, this *slut*?"

Rain shook angrily and stood up before he replied. "Yes mom, but she's beautiful...no gorgeous. You're just an ugly BITCH!"

She crossed the room and slapped her son viciously, knocking him to the floor. "To think, of what I *sacrificed* for you. This is what I get?! This is the thanks you give me?!"

She turned to Sabrina. "You're fired cunt. Get the fuck out of here."

"NO MOM!"

"SHUT the hell up Rain. You're being punished."

He began crying and April just ignored him. "Stop crying, I didn't do anything wrong. You *messed* up."

 His father came in and after a few moments of whispering to April, ushered her from the room. He helped Rain get up and handed him a towel to clean off. He bitterly smiled, waiting for his son to change to clean clothes while he sat on the edge of the bed. Rain closed his bedroom door and sat next to his father. He could tell that the aging process was not being kind. Doug's hair was graying or falling out, his face lined with wrinkles and his hands shook.

"Are you okay son?"

"How can I be OK? April just *slapped* me for jerking off?!"

"Yeah, I'm sorry she did that. You shouldn't have egged her on, but she still shouldn't have hit you. I'm sorry."
There was an awkward silence between them that lasted nearly a minute. Rain didn't dare speak, he could tell his father was thinking about what he was going to say next.

"See April doesn't get that Gutermuth's ages you, both in body and mind. In fact, I'd guess you're more like 16 than 14 now. She should have expected this. After all…you're a young man now and Sabrina is an attractive woman."
Rain looked down, embarrassed.

"Anyways, don't listen to her Rain. She's wrong. You have nothing to be ashamed of. While I'm slightly bothered that your nanny was your "first pick", I can't fault you for that. Who else do you see when you spend all your time up here?"

"No one." Rain whispered.

"That's right. So don't feel ashamed for being attracted to her. Just try to be more *discrete*."

"I guess…"

"All right. That'll do." He kissed Rain gently on the forehead. "I love you."

"I love you too dad."

Doug smiled at that, getting up and making to leave. Just before he exited the room however, he turned back. "Just make sure this mess is gone in the morning. No need for your mother to see it twice right?"

Rain smiled. "Ok."

Doug left and Rain considered his words. It was somewhat comforting, but April's bile and the stinging sensation of her slap left stayed with him. He felt ashamed and humiliated, just less so thanks to his dad. He buried his face in his pillow and began crying, turning it dark grey.

Lily awoke tired, after having another restless night. Isaac had collapsed a few days ago and she still wasn't sure why. After he had been brought into the intensive care unit, she was cut off from him. They insisted that only family members could know his condition. She also knew that they remembered that he had *none*. It was just a legal formality and it made Lily's stomach turn. She was so worried for him, not only was he nice to her, but she really liked him. He was her only friend in this place. Maybe her only friend ever, because her mother had tried to leash her, Vicky was a machine and Abby had mixed motives in being concerned for her.

She got up, her body feeling heavy and her mood dampened. She noticed a handwritten note, stuffed awkwardly underneath her door. So, the isolation room had a flaw or two. She picked it up and began smiling. It was from Isaac! Apparently, he was feeling better and was waiting for her in the playroom. Her heart began racing. He was okay! She quickly exited her room, wondering what surprise he had for her in the playroom. She strolled through the halls quickly, ignoring the concerned and irritated glances of the hospital staff. When she arrived, the blinds were down and the lights dimmed.

Oh what could it be! She jumped up and down excitedly, the anticipation forcing her to rekey the password a few times. She entered the room, getting sprayed with disinfectants and sealing both doors behind her. She searched for Isaac in the gloom. What was he going to do? Try and scare her? Turn on the lights suddenly and shout surprise? She stopped looking suddenly, seeing Francis emerge. He had a wicked smile and her blood ran cold. He began approaching her and she turned away, running back towards the door. Then Hernan appeared from behind her and raised one of game boards above his head. She made to scream, but Francis grabbed her from behind. He put tape over her mouth and pinned her arms back.

She watched terrified as Hernan smashed the board

against the inner access panel and sealed them inside the room. Now neither doors would open, unless someone keyed in the manual override password on the outside. She swallowed nervously, wanting to know why they wanted to trap her here. Her gut twisted as Hernan turned to her, finished with his task. He wore a smug smile of satisfaction and knew immediately that whatever it was that they wanted from her, they had planned for it. He began speaking, his words taking on a menacing tone as Francis' breaths grew shallower.

"Lily, I don't imagine a girl like you is going to understand what's about to happen, but that only makes it better. Being cut off from the world and all. That said, no one is coming to save you, not even Isaac. We poisoned him and he won't be functional for several more days if he's lucky enough to survive. We slowly added things to his regular diet that poisoned him and it will take the doctors some time to figure that part out, since his body built a steady tolerance…to a point…"

Lily swallowed nervously, understanding only part of it. She felt an icy shiver run down her spine.

"Now we've lowered the naptime blinds, covered the cameras with toys and now…now we're going to *rape* you."

 Rape? What was that? She had no idea what the word meant, but Hernan wore a dark smile. The face of someone looking to kill, like one of the many men

Agent Yi fought. Lily began struggling against Francis and nearly wriggled out of his grasp when Hernan savagely punched her face. There were stars in her eyes and a red, pulsing welt on her face. She fell the ground and barely registered the words the two uttered.

"Why did you do that? Now she's uglier."

"Shut the fuck up. She nearly got away, you weakling. We're taking her from behind anyway. This is the *only* chance we'll ever get with a girl. Grab her by the pussy…"

They picked her up and pinned her against the table, the hard, wooden surface jutting awkwardly against her belly. She cried out from the pain, but the tape muted her. She felt her hospital gown being lifted and her underwear pulled to the floor. Then he shoved something inside her, inside that hole Other talked about. He took her brutishly, thrusting against her with maniacal glee. She cried out and tried to struggle free, but Francis had pinned her hands on the table while Hernan had gripped her body in a tight lock. She felt fiery pain erupt from within her, as Hernan's movements increased. She felt possessed, Hernan running his fingers through her hair while muttering in Spanish. Francis watched from across the table with a dark smile of admiration and reached downwards with his right hand.

She continued to struggle, but her body grew weak and exhausted her reserves of energy. She felt that

Hernan had practically become a part of her. The part of him entering and exiting her had stiffened over time and fit the hole better. Still, she began crying only to the pleasure of Hernan.

"Yes! Suffer puta! It only makes me harder!"

When she nearly felt the will to fight gone, the Other appeared. She glared at Lily and began shouting.

"Fight you dumb bitch! You didn't listen to Vicky, your mother or even Abby! How can you let this savage take you like this when Isaac loves you?!"
  Lily stopped crying, Other was right. Isaac loved her and she had let this buffoon, this monster violate her. She clenched her fists and tightened her thighs, renewing her struggle.

"Eh? You still have some fight in you? I like that." He said cruelly, kissing the good side of her face. "Its…" He stopped mid-sentence as something struck the room's windows.

"Francis go check that out!" Hernan ordered.

  Francis ignored him, Lily could tell he was invested in pleasuring himself. Hernan slapped him and then Francis obeyed. He walked over to the glass and Lily took her chance. She pushed off from the table and escaped a surprised Hernan's grasp. She finally realized how sore her groin and stomach were, but Hernan knocked her to the floor. She ripped the tape off however and began wildly struggling. It was messy, but it kept Hernan from getting a grip on her.

Then a chair crashed through the window, hitting Francis with several shards of glass and knocking him down. Lily wrestled with Hernan on the floor, feeling glass shards pinprick her multiple times. Other watched, smiling darkly as Isaac strode over and threw Hernan off her. He dropped the note the two gave her.

"Its over Hernan. Stop. Now." He commanded.

"NO its not!" He said, rushing at them.

She briefly saw his face, an animalistic expression contorted with anger and shock. She kicked him in the gut while Isaac clocked him. He got up again however, holding a large piece of glass. He slashed at them with it. While Isaac struggled to stop him from slashing her throat, Other spoke to her.
"Pick up the glass and kill Hernan and Francis. It's the only way you're getting out alive."
She hesitated, but only for a moment. Her face also contorted in an dark rage. She couldn't violate him, but she could take his life. She picked up a large shard of glass and stabbed Hernan several times with it, only relenting once his face went slack and a pool of blood coated the floor. Francis then pounced on her, knocking her to the ground.

"He was my friend! Fuck you bitch!" He said, as he began beating her.

Isaac wore a shocked face but intervened, punching Francis in the head. As Francis shook his head in pain, she slashed the glass against his throat and he collapsed. Blood soaked her clothes. She pushed him off and Isaac stared at her with a dull terror. He walked off, unable to speak and vomited on the floor. Lily looked at what she did, curling and shaking as the adrenaline wearing off. Other stared at her gleefully and said,

"Now, you're a woman. April, Vicky and Abby have no power over you." Other touched her bruised face gently and she briefly saw the suit Other wore materialize over her ruined gown. Lily screamed.

Chapter V.

April cried into her lawyer's shoulders just outside the courtroom. When she had first heard the news, she nearly fainted. Lily had been raped…by two boys! She only survived because she and another boy killed the rapists. Her baby had been *violated* by those…those monsters! All because that *cunt* Abby used legalese to overrule her and exposed Lily. She eventually stopped crying, anger taking over. Yes, she would let the jury and justice see a hurt, crying mother while Abby would only know her wrath! She burst into the courtroom, rushing past the shocked onlookers to her seat and, noting with some satisfaction, that they all looked embarrassed.

She turned to the left, seeing one of the women she most hated, almost more than Abby. Sabrina. She sat there watching her, hurt and intelligence in those eyes. April sneered back. So, years after their settlement, she returned to haunt April once more. She glared at the woman as Abby called her to the stand. Were they going to try justifying the crime she committed? If so, this would be interesting and would assure April's success in the case.

"Sabrina Robinson, I know that you have already settled with April previously, but your role in this case is particularly *unique*. Can you briefly explain your part of it?" Abby asked.

"Yes…yes I can. Its why I'm here today. It's truly and unbelievably tragic what happened to that girl. Believe me, the guilt I feel for what I did is real and painful. Still, I did it because I loved April's son, Rain. I was his babysitter at first, but I could tell immediately that he was older than he appeared. He pursued me, quite obsessively at first and I yielded to him mostly out of pity. Still, he showed me how a person can endure something as terrible as Gutermuth's and even find love and happiness. I still paid for my choices and he died regardless." She finished, tearing up as she looked at the jury.

"You paid with my husband's money!" April retorted.

Steele glared at her and said, "Ms. Green you will remain quiet while Abby questions her witnesses. Otherwise, you will be thrown out of this courtroom."

She nodded reluctantly, trying to resist the urge to spit at the man.

"I see, can you just clarify what you did for Rain then?"

"I started working at the Thompson Clinic and I helped him donate some sperm a few times, stealing the academic records of top-tier college students that had disappeared or died so that his sperm would be more valuable."

"Why did you do this?"

"I did it because he asked me too and he was addicted to painkillers. So he needed the money." She turned to the jury. "See, Gutermuth's slowly hollows you out from the inside. It systematically destroys your body and leaves you older, weaker and more helpless until you finally die. Rain never wanted any of that so he took heroin and cocaine to avoid feeling that decay inside of him. Unfortunately, his tolerance for the drugs only grew until he overdosed."

"Thank you Sabrina. I have no further questions. Would you like to interrogate the witness?" Abby asked April.

She turned to her lawyer briefly and shook her head. Her anger had gone cold and there was nothing she could get from it. In the eyes of the law, Sabrina had paid for her crime.

"I call Dr. Jakob to the stand."

April began shaking and her lawyer did his best to reassure her. That bastard was here too! Had Abby dug out all of her skeletons? She still thought she could win! Well, that cunt would be proven wrong quickly. You can't get away with raping little girls!

Justice Steele interrupted her. "Mrs. Dunkel, I fail to see the relevance of this man's testimony to the case. You and your client disavowed him years ago, starting this whole mess. He also lost his medical license and the title doctor is no longer fitting. I think it is time we move to the new development in the case. Your use of the Dunkel Precedent was on shaky grounds and it resulted in Lily getting raped. I think it is your turn to testify."

April's lawyer nodded and called her to the stand.

Inside, April was seething. Abby might have been legally Mrs. Dunkel, but April was married to Doug for almost fifteen years. Abby got lucky to have a little over two years with him. She also noticed that Jakob had sat down and was remaining silent. Thompson had probably paid him off and now he wouldn't even have to lie during his testimony. April recoiled at that thought.

"Mrs. Dunkel…er Abby…" He corrected. "Why did you use the Dunkel Precedent to emancipate Lily from April's preferred treatment? You had a conflict of interest in the case, did not legally represent Lily and she is legally my client's daughter not yours."

 She hesitated for a few moments, but sighed and answered. "I did it to spite April for all the suffering she caused me and Doug. I also found Lily to be so hopeful and bright. So, it was heartbreaking to see how she was dying under April's strict supervision. Now…though, I see that there are many subtle gradations between being free and controlled. She got raped because of that and I'll have to learn to live with my choices."
April snorted, but said nothing, sensing defeat.

"I think it's time we settle this. Don't you Abby? I mean we've already imperiled this girl's life and spent so much time on this case." Steele said calmly.

Abby looked to the Thompson representative, whom reluctantly nodded. April smiled inwardly, at least it was finally over.

"However, I am adding a caveat in light of this development April. Lily will have a continuous psychological evaluation every three months for the next three years. If abuse is found, Lily may be taken from you. Is that understood?"
April momentarily felt anger well up inside her. She quelled it though and replied.

"Understood."

Suddenly a man burst into the courtroom and April turned to look at him. He was some dirty old spic in ratty clothes and he began yelling.

"No. How can the death of mi hijo mean nada!"
April's blood ran cold. He was Hernan's father. She stood up and addressed the man. "Fuck you Spic! Your son raped my daughter. He got what he deserved."

"No, he was just a lonely boy and he did something stupid. The staff should have kept better track of Lily!" He insisted.

"WHAT?!" April shouted, rushing over to the man and savagely starting to beat him. Steele yelled for order as the bailiff grabbed her, blood coating her hands and the old bastard lying unconscious on the floor. As he dragged April away, she glared at Steele and cursed wildly.

The hospital staff informed her that her mother won the case with Thompson. Lily was also well enough to finally go home. Well enough in body perhaps, but not in mind. Lily touched her vagina, learning what it was it called and what it was from the doctors. It still felt raw and violated. Other and a version of Twin clothed in a hospital gown stood there, saying nothing. At least Other looked sympathetic, Twin wore an awkward face. She had been raped and her mother was taking her home. She escaped one hell and went into another. Worse of all, she was going to have to endure it without Isaac. She started crying. The boy had risked his life to save her.

As if on cue, he appeared outside her door. He entered her room too, under the watchful supervision of the staff. Other and Twin disappeared.

"H…Hi Lily…"
"Isaac…" She said, reaching out.

He backed away. "I'm sorry. The doctors said I can't touch you. They said it was your mom's orders."
She grimaced. "Ok…let's talk then."
He nodded happily, but didn't continue the conversation. He seemed put out, maybe he was embarrassed or afraid of offending her.

"Isaac. It's okay to speak plainly with me. Without you, I probably would have died at Hernan's and Francis' hands."
He relaxed a little. "I just wish I had gotten there sooner and stopped them from doing anything to you. I also…*wish* that I had the courage to kill them. I should have taken that burden from you."

"Isaac…" She said softly. "You were sickened by them

and did all you could. I'll appreciate that forever and I…I *love* you Isaac."
He didn't speak or move for several seconds. He looked shocked.

"I l…love you too Lily." He stammered.

  She smiled and drew him in for a big kiss. He struggled for a few moments, but then enjoyed it. However, she saw the staff rushing in and opening the door.
"I guess this is goodbye." She said. Then her mother appeared. She began kicking and screaming as the hospital staff grabbed her, bringing her to April.

  April stared angrily at her as she struggled. However, she stopped screaming and saw Isaac trying to speak. She saw him mouth something, but couldn't tell what it was. She started crying again.

  Rain sipped at his ice-cold soda idly, wondering where Sabrina was. She finally agreed to go on a date with him, probably out of pity. Still, he had the confidence to ask her, because he was finally free. Dad divorced April and won most of the custody rights. After 15 years of an unhappy marriage, they finally split a year ago. Rain couldn't be happier as the divorce finalized today. Even though his mother made the initial choice to keep him, he had grown closer to his father.

  They shared the decay and exhaustion from the disease, which mellowed out his father and made April more bitter. She wanted more control and more power over her husband and son, but she could never understand. She wasn't born with a slow, agonizing death sentence. He casually slipped some cocaine powder into his drink, letting it soothe his weary body and soul. He appreciated that his father provided him with it, even if he didn't want him using it. As he closed his eyes and enjoyed the feelings, Sabrina tapped the table and awoke him from his reverie. She quickly ordered a water and turned back to him.

"Hi Rain. How are you?"

He smiled. She looked radiant. Her dark hair was neatly combed and her blue eyes accentuated by her pale mascara. She wore a simple blue dress, unbuttoned down to mid-chest.

"I'm…I'm well, thank you. You?"

"I'm well. I just heard from your father that the divorce papers finally came through. Do you want to talk about it?"

"No, not really. My feelings on my mother are quite clear. Don't you remember what happened when I was 14?"

"All too well, its burned into my memory. It's certainly why it's a bit awkward being here. Is this something…of a dream come true for you?" She asked honestly.

"I suppose you could say that. Still, don't think of it that way. You're the only woman I've really met and known, outside of my mother."

"What about the other babysitters? Didn't you spend time getting to know them?"

"No, my mother insisted on only male candidates that passed her rigorous background checks. My father didn't tell you?"

"No, he left that detail out. I suppose he was embarrassed."

"Well anyone would be by April. She's a headstrong, emotional woman who works to get what she wants, damned what others want."

"Still, she's your mother. You must have some feelings for her, right?"

"Other than hatred and shame, I have none." He coldly insisted.

"Oh come on…you still love her on some level. I mean she chose to keep you."

"Yes and that decision will haunt me for as long as I live. Sometimes…I wonder if it was better that I had never been *born*."

"Don't say that. Sure, your average lifespan is shorter than mine, but that doesn't mean it must be. Just look at your father!"

"I do, I see more of myself in him every day. Both the good and the *bad*. I have his intelligence, but his underlying despair too. Anyone with Gutermuth's would know that feeling of existential dread of death."

"Still, you're smarter and more mature than anyone I've ever met your age."

"And at what cost? I get to be older in mind and body, living shorter lives than my peers. What good is that?!"

"Well…you're alive and you're here for however long

you get. I think I'm going to go Rain. This was a mistake. Your father's dying too, but he isn't as bitter about it."

She got up to leave.
"Wait, I apologize Sabrina. You're right. This is our first date and I should have been…more *polite*. I just don't have much experience doing this sort of thing. Please… forgive me."

"Fine…I won't ask you about your mother again. I see how touchy you are about it."
   The words stung, but he swallowed his pride. "I think I love my mother deep down, but it's a twisted love. It's filled with longing, regret, shame and hatred. I can't really distinguish my feelings too clearly."
"I see. I apologize then. I think I've been spoiled by my home life. Not much melodrama there."
"Well then…you must be a boring person deep down." He replied snarkly.

"Shut the fuck up. Let's order some food. All this *talk* has made me hungry."
He smiled and gestured the waiter over to them.

   Lily was finally home after several months away. She had changed so much, but she noted that home had not. Vicky remained a logical, imperturbable machine and her mother still resented her independence. How could she understand? She was not raped nor endured years of submission. Well, Lily would not submit anymore. Still, she would be more patient and cautious this time. April also refused to reveal the reasons behind the court case with Thompson, stating it was none of her business. How dare she?! Lily would find out the truth this time and no illness would stop her efforts.

If the truth was anywhere, it was hidden in her mother's room. So she made preparations the last few nights that would allow her entry. She collected a plastic utensil and sharpened it in the bathroom while she bathed. She did her best to recollect how Hernan disabled the door's keypad, despite being haunted by the memories. Next, she enabled the adult settings on Vicky while it was in sleep mode last night. Lastly, she viciously argued with her mother. She had not noticed the change in the morning, so Lily had succeeded in distracting and exhausting her. Lily put Vicky in sleep mode and walked over to her mother's bedroom, passing the playset. She felt a momentary burst of childish excitement, but it quickly dissipated. She had to know the truth and she would know it now. She tried prying open the metal keypad with her sharpened tool, failing to break it and cutting herself instead.

After washing the wound with hydrogen peroxide and applying a bandage, she returned. She knew that Vicky could open the door remotely, but that would be recorded and her mother would know she broke in. She wanted to avoid that *argument*. Instead, she remembered a trick Agent Yi used to break into the Politburo headquarters. She searched the kitchen and found a clean fingerprint on the coffeemaker. She grabbed some tape and carefully peeled the fingerprint off. She returned to the door and gently applied the tape to the scanner. After a few moments of verifying, it opened and she entered.

The room was still generally clean, but there were signs of April's distress. Forgotten articles of clothing, wrinkles in the bedsheets and several papers on the floor. She began reading them, quickly searching for something related to Thompson. Then she found it: a letter from a clinic employee named Dr. William Jakob. It listed the results of a paternity test April had commissioned. It said things like the birth was improbable and that Lily inherited Gutermuth's by chance. It included an official apology from Thompson over the actions of a Rain Dunkel and Sabrina Robinson. It showed his name, her mother's name and hers. It was wrong though, listing her as Lily Green not Lily Dunkel. She didn't understand, why was the letter so wrong? What was a paternity test? She had to look this Rain person up. She took the letter with her to her bedroom and activated her tablet.

Rain started shaking, his withdrawal was growing worse. His father insisted that he stop taking so much cocaine, but it was too late for that. He was dying and he had at most five years left. So he needed money to purchase drug to ease his pain, but he couldn't safely hold a job being very sick and an addict. So he came with a brilliant idea, but Sabrina opposed it initially.

He eventually wore her down and now she helped the scheme. She got a job with the Thompson Clinic and would fake his records so that he could donate sperm for money. However, after collecting it and registering it, she would destroy the sample and pay him regardless. That way, he wouldn't father any Gutermuth's babies, but he could also make the money he desperately needed.

He sat in the clinic, patiently reading a magazine while Sabrina prepped the back room for him. It was another tasteless one with a scantily-clad woman on the front page, designed to get you into the mood and buy the magazine. He smiled inwardly, despite its crassness, it worked. Sabrina peered over the top of the magazine and said,

"Come with me sir. The room is ready for you."

He nodded, doing his best to disguise his excitement. He was about to make good money and…Sabrina, she looked so good. The gentle lab coat did little to hide her curves. He imagined other donors thought the same. They entered the room, filled with lots of pornographic material. However, he wasn't going to use any of that. He and Sabrina would just do a quickie. Instead of shooting out onto the floor, he would do it into a cup.

She locked the door and kissed him strongly, making heart flutter. She snaked her hands down his pants, unbuckling his belt while stroking him. He removed her lab coat carefully, making sure not to rip out a button. He pushed a breast out of her bra, kissing it fiercely while she pulled down his boxers. He slipped the condom over quickly and pinned her against the couch, slipping off her panties and removing her bra. He thrusted into her, being sure not to come or be too loud. He smiled inwardly, remembering their many failed practice sessions. As his hands tightened around her waist, her breaths grew shallow and she closed her eyes. She lightly moaned as he quickened. He tensed, feeling the orgasmic rush building. He exited her, panting rapidly as he inserted his penis into the collection cup. As she caught her breath, he exploded into it three times, a wave of ecstasy rising within him. That done, she sealed the cup and placed it on the table, getting dressed and making to leave. He stopped her, pinning her on the couch again. He would not leave until she orgasmed as well. He dove down, her face again contorting with delight.

Lily typed Rain Dunkel in her tablet, initially finding little. There was an old obituary about a teenager's tragic death due to overdose and some divorce proceedings. Both were over a decade old. She considered both webpages and saw April and Doug's names mentioned both times. The obituary listed Rain as their son. *Rain…*he was her brother. Her older, dead brother. Why had April hidden this from her? Why was he listed in the letter from Dr. Jakob? Her gut twisted up, but she pushed on. Her mind was finally piecing it together.

She looked up the phrase 'paternity test' and shook badly as she read the medical definition: "*a medical test, typically a blood test, to determine whether a man may be the father of a particular child.*" No! That couldn't be true! Surely, it wasn't true. She ran to the kitchen and turned on Vicky, screaming.

"TELL ME! Tell me Rain isn't my father!" She said, holding the letter up to the camera.

The machine activated slowly, speaking to her in a monotone.
"I'm afraid I can't do that Lily. Rain Dunkel is your father. Now, you need to calm down and breathe. I can play some smooth jazz to help you relax." It began playing.

"NO, no! Stop that. I don't want to calm down!" Her head was spinning.

"Lily. You *must* calm down or you'll fail your psychiatric evaluation in a few days…"
"Wait, what?!"

"Yes, you'll be visiting with a court-appointed doctor in a few days. Has April not discussed this with you?"

A court-ordered psych eval? Her mother would hide this from her. She would hide anything inconvenient or troubling from her. Well screw her and screw Vicky. No one was going to tell her what to feel or hide the truth any longer. She grabbed her tablet and rapidly smashed it against Vicky's interface. She ignored the machine's pleas to stop until it crashed onto the floor, unrepairable. She cut herself in the process, glass from the tablet embedded in her hands and arms. She distantly noted the blood slowly spilling out of her, the shape of the cuts. She fell to the ground, shaking uncontrollably. She was the child of her mother and dead brother. How?! Why?! She didn't want to know. She couldn't know…*unless* it was probably Thompson's doing.

He probably donated his seed there and April received it, resulting in herself. She cried as the shaking intensified. Why her? What had she done wrong? Then she realized it, she only existed because of April's selfishness. April must have circumvented the laws on Gutermuth's and tried being impregnated by a clean donor. Lily laughed darkly, but life wasn't so nice to April. She had a child, a child with Gutermuth's born of her dead son. Lily only suffered because of April's selfish choices.

She got up, knowing suddenly what she had to do. She would screw April over with one final act. She would no longer suffer at her hands! Lily's life was just a long, slow death. A continuation of an unending hell until she finally died. She wouldn't go through that though, no not if April forced her to. She walked over to the bathroom, blood dripping from her forearms. She turned on the bathtub, filling it with warm water rapidly as the machine could no longer stop her. She threw off her clothes and dipped into it. She was at peace. She picked a piece of glass from her arm, slashing it against both of her arms and cutting deep. She closed her eyes, the pain and suffering leaving her.

She imagined floating over an empty ocean as the bathwater turned red.

April panicked as she tried opening the door, finding the keypad unresponsive. Vicky was broken. She knew it! Why though? Her mind flickered through potential reasons, none of them comforting. She activated the manual override for the door, pushing against a panel in the right place. She ignored the decontamination protocols, the machine was broken anyway and Lily was certainly in trouble. Vicky's updates stopped over an hour ago and its last one was a garbled mess of Lily screaming.

She opened the apartment door, finding it eerily quiet. There was a mess in the kitchen: a broken Vicky, glass everywhere and blood. April started shaking and followed the blood trails to the bathroom. She swallowed, slowly opening the door.

"Lily…"

She gasped and rushed over to the bathtub, its reddish water spilling. Lily's body was cold and the cuts on her arm slowly oozed blood. She checked for a pulse and pumped Lily's chest for a minute. It failed and April knew she was dead. She started crying and whimpering.

"Lily…my sweet…please…NO! WHY?!"

April brushed back Lily's hair and cradled her lifeless body. She looked so much like herself, at least when she younger. She cried harder, tears dropping into the water rapidly. She failed once again, her baby was gone. This time though, there was no second chance. Her womb was as lifeless as her family was. She released the corpse and sat against the bathtub, weeping loudly.

April cradled her growing belly and smiled. She was three months pregnant and everything was going smoothly. She wasn't going to make the same mistakes she did with Rain. She bought a new apartment, an entire floor even in a new complex to raise her child in peace. She was too old to deal with the stresses of neighbors and was never particularly sociable. In addition, she had something new to watch over her child while she worked. There would be no repeats of Ms. Robinson. Nor would the outside world or an unhappy marriage corrupt the child. She would raise it on her own, no matter the difficulties.

She sat, gently touching the leather sofa. It smelled fresh and gave her hope as she considered the choices of the last few months. Dr. Jakob and the Thompson Clinic kindly provided the sperm she needed. Her loss was not forever. They overlooked the laws against it, albeit only with sufficient financial incentive. Now she waited for the results of the early medical screenings. Hopefully, they would assuage her nerves.

She got up and walked over to the kitchen, unpacking the VHA and reading the box. She named it Victoria, the name she wanted to give Rain if he had turned out to be a girl. She carefully memorized the instructions and followed them through. She drilled holes in the wall to attach the VHA to and gently put it into place. She typed in her preferred settings and activated the machine when the doorbell rang. She clenched her fists. Apparently, she would need to add an elevator key to prevent people from going to her floor. There was only one apartment on it, which was listed in the elevator. She briskly walked over to the door and opened it, her jaw dropping. It was Doug.

"Hello April, may I come in?"

"*Why?*"

"Well the doctors told me I only have a few months left. I wanted to see you and just…*talk.*"

 She grimaced. Despite the years of separation and the pain they caused each other, she still had some feelings for him. Not much, but something.

"Ok, but take your shoes off and be careful. It's a new apartment and I'd rather not scuff it up so soon."
He smiled weakly and obliged. "It looks beautiful. You've done well for yourself."
She smiled politely and ushered him into the living room. When they both sat down, she asked,

"Doug, what do you want to talk about?"

"Gosh…so many things…I know it's been too long though. I'll be concise."
She nodded.

"Firstly though, how's work?"
"Its fine. I just thought of this new idea that might just get the company to notice my talents."
"What is it?"

"It's a…uh artificial womb."
"Really? What made you think of that?"

"Well, our experiences Doug. The difficulty of having a healthy child, especially with the fear of genetic flaws. An artificial womb would better control for the genes of a child, even more than in-vitro."

Doug's eyebrows furrowed. "Isn't that still a long way off though?"
"Yes, the uterus is not something we can easily replicate. Still, an early model could be used to grow embryonic tissue or something for medical research."

"I see…"
"How about you? How's work?"

"I…retired a few months ago. My time at Anson is finally over."
"It was a long career…what like twenty years?"

"Yes…yes it was…"
"Any *regrets*?"

"No…not really. I did well there. Wait…are you talking about Abby?"

"Well, who else?" She replied, glaring.

"OK, I admit I was weak during our marriage and…I'm sorry for cheating on you with Abby.

But…every day we were married, we hurt each other
April. We were unhappy together."
"We were only *unhappy*, because you couldn't handle
raising a son with Gutermuth's."
"I never wanted to. I stated that at the beginning. You
held me hostage and forced me to choose between you
and the child or being alone while dying from a
disease. That's no choice at all."

"Still, fuck you for cheating on me. You should have
had the balls to divorce me then."
"Well, I would have…but I grew attached to Rain. I
sympathized with his struggle and knew it intimately.
I couldn't abandon him. So I tried working things out
with you. I knew what he meant to you. I stayed as
long as I could April…"

"You fucked up Rain, you know that? You poisoned
him with your bitterness. You contributed to his *death*."
"I'll admit, I played a part in his overdose, but you had
a role too. You wanted absolute control over his life
and mine. You made him paranoid and made him take
whatever happiness he could. He took drugs. So yeah,
I facilitated his decline. You started it, by humiliating
him for jerking off!"

"Shut up! Get out!" She started crying.

"Shit…fuck I'm sorry. God…I didn't want to come
here and do this…"
"Just *GO*."

"Ok, I'll just say this. Congrats on the pregnancy. I
really mean it. I know why you did it, despite the risk

and the efforts I've made in the past. I hope that you took proper precautions though and remember what happened to our family. Admit your flaws and let the child help you grow, otherwise they'll turn out just like Rain."

He left. April continued to cry, burying her face in her hands.

  April checked her emails one last time, deliberately avoiding all the letters of consolation. Her coworkers never took an interest in her life before, so it was infuriating that they did now. She noticed one from Mr. Barrett however and opened it tentatively.

Dear April,

I find it difficult to find words to say. I realize now that I have been insensitive about your situation and I'll admit that I honestly forgot about it. I can't imagine what it's like to lose a child nor can I offer you much words of comfort. I lost my family too for similar reasons, but many of those I think were ultimately selfish. My own children have lived separate lives from me for decades and I was never really a father to them. I imagine you felt the same at times, being so busy, and wonder if your sacrifices to our company were worth it.

Unfortunately, that is for you to decide. I do hope that you'll continue to work here at Williamson, but we won't hold it against you if you don't. I do want to congratulate you on the artificial womb project though, it appears to be quite successful and is making significant headway. While it might be decades before we grow actual babies inside of them, the growth of embryonic tissue for medical research will certainly be profitable. The board will continue to fund the project and I expect great things from you, April.

If you need time to grieve and rest, please take a few weeks off and then return to us. We'll be waiting for you. If that's not enough, good luck with everything.

Best,

James Barrett

CEO, Williamson Corporation

She was stunned, Mr. Barrett took the time to write something heartfelt to her. It had to be, it was too revealing to be written by a member of his staff. She wanted to feel good about that, but she couldn't. Instead, she got out of her car and put the phone away. She would return to work in a few weeks, but there wasn't really a reason to work anymore besides money. The cold January winds bristled against her coat and she pulled it tighter to her body. The cemetery was empty, freshly cleaned of snow. She walked through its narrow, salted pathways, each bootstep crunching beneath her.

She arrived at their graves, a single tear falling to the ground. She knelt, gingerly touching each tombstone: Rain Dunkel, Doug Dunkel and Lily Green. She was the only one left of her family. She stifled a sob, placing an iris, a rose and a lily on their graves respectively. She collapsed to the ground, with no desire to move. She had tried so hard to keep her family together, but failed due to her mistakes and the cruelty of the universe. She grabbed a bottle of champagne from her purse and began drinking it, anger and despair welling within her.

 It should have been a special day today, but it wasn't. Instead, she just turned 51. She wanted to feel some excitement, but there was only a tightness in her chest. She laughed emptily and offered a mock toast to her family. To the Dunkels, may they forever rest in peace. She continued laughing, the cold wind drawing out her tears. She gulped down the rest of the wine and rested her head against Doug's tombstone. She whispered,

"You were right…I'm sorry. I'm so sorry…"

About the Author

Karl Diaz is an experienced communicator in multiple formats: personal, email, phone. He has experience with Facebook and Twitter, promoting two events with two hundred plus participants. He is a passionate, community-focused collaborator, with a focus on environmental, social justice and equity issues. He has worked with nonprofit, academic and government entities.

As a program assistant for George Mason's Office of Local Government and Community Relations, he promoted the 2016 Go Gaga for Green event. He did so through social media, emails, phone calls and personal meetings. It celebrated environmentally-conscious individuals in Northern Virginia and Arlington County public school students. He organized Operation Rain Barrel, calling schools to check progress of their rain barrels and to ensure timely delivery before the event. These barrels taught students about the importance of water conservation and were sold at the event.

He then worked for <u>Arlingtonians for a Clean Environment</u> in summer 2016. He answered calls, sent emails and summarized an academic survey of fifth to eighth graders' environmental knowledge. Following that, he worked as a volunteer for the <u>Sierra Club's Ready for 100 campaign</u>, advocating the adoption of 100% renewable electricity in Arlington by 2035.

He graduated from <u>George Mason</u> with a Bachelor of Arts in Environmental and Sustainable Studies in fall 2016. He then interned for <u>Senate of Virginia</u> for <u>Senator Jeremy McPike</u> in spring 2017. He attended committee meetings, helped track the senator's bills, attended bill hearings, answered constituents on the phone and through email and responded to letters sent to the Senator.

In summer 2017, he actively promoted <u>Resilient Virginia's annual conference</u>. He ran the social media campaign through Facebook and Twitter, contacted prospective attendees, organized the speakers and provided on-hand assistance at the event.

Lastly in fall 2017, he volunteered with <u>Groundwork RVA.</u> He maintained <u>Bellemeade Community Center</u> by weeding, mowing, and mulching. He also worked on recycling bins for the Highland Park neighborhood, built a greenhouse and filmed a recycling promotion video.

He is actively searching for his first job in the

environmental advocacy field.

In terms of writing, his focus is on science fiction, environmental, bioethics and social issues.

His favorite science-fiction genres include near-future, alternate history, space opera and social-science.

www.ingramcontent.com/pod-product-compliance
Lightning Source LLC
Chambersburg PA
CBHW060941050726
47592CB00003B/1051